THE
N RMAL
KID

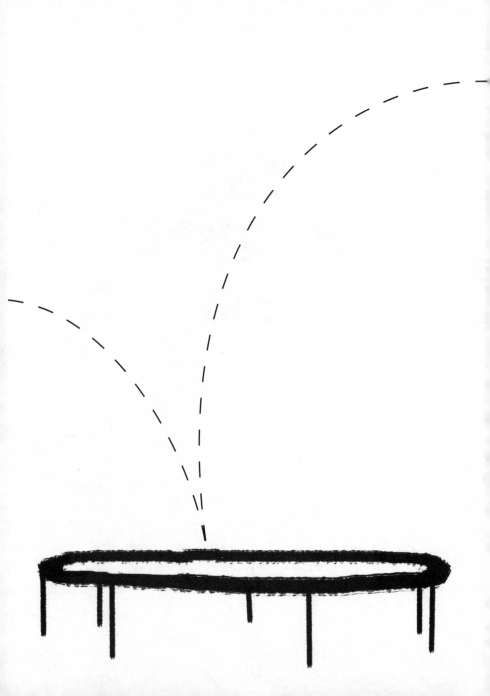

THE N☺RMAL KID

Elizabeth Holmes

Carolrhoda Books • Minneapolis

Carolrhoda Books
A division of Lerner Publishing Group, Inc.
241 First Avenue North
Minneapolis, MN 55401 U.S.A.

Website address: www.lernerbooks.com

Cover background © iStockphoto.com/Rich Seymour.

Library of Congress Cataloging-in-Publication Data

Holmes, Elizabeth, 1957–
        The normal kid / by Elizabeth Holmes.
            p.   cm.
        Summary: Told in their separate voices, fifth–graders Sylvan, whose parents' divorce causes him stress, and Charity, who lived in Kenya for the past five years, both strive for normalcy at school and start a petition to keep their teacher, Mr. In, from being fired.
        ISBN 978–0–7613–8085–6 (trade hard cover : alk. paper)
        [1. Schools—Fiction. 2. Individuality—Fiction. 3. Moving, Household—Fiction. 4. Divorce—Fiction. 5. Faith—Fiction. 6. Family life—New York (State)—Fiction. 7. New York (State)—Fiction.] I. Title.
PZ7.H7355Nor 2012
[Fic]—dc23   2011046589

Manufactured in the United States of America
1 – SB – 7/15/12

chapter one

SYLVAN

There are two weird kids in my class this year, and they're two totally different kinds of weird. One is Charity Jensen, who has spent almost her whole life in Africa. The other one—well, everybody calls him the Trampoline Kid.

My name is Sylvan, and I am a normal kid.

· · · · ·

At the start of fifth grade, it didn't take long to figure out who the weird kids were. That was pretty clear by the end of the first day.

Like the Trampoline Kid. I know his name now—Brian Laidlaw—but I still think of him as the Trampoline Kid. That's because I was watching him all summer even though I didn't know him. He must have just moved into the yellow house that's a block and a half from mine. There were never any kids in that house before. And I never saw a trampoline there. But one day last July I walked by, and a huge trampoline was set up. It had a net all around it like a fence, so you couldn't fall off.

Every time I walked by, this kid was out there bouncing. He had really light hair—almost white. He usually wore the same T-shirt, a gray one with a green and orange frog on it. Sometimes he had his arms down flat against his sides, launching himself like a rocket. Sometimes he flopped to his knees or flat on his back, and then bounced up and landed on his feet.

I'd walk by real slow, hoping he'd invite me to try it. I'd walk by pretty often too, because his house was on the way if I was going to the little grocery store or my friend Adam's house.

Sometimes I walked over there just to see if he was out on the trampoline. He usually was.

This kid looked about my age, and there was never anyone else bouncing with him, so I couldn't see why he didn't invite me. I know he saw me. His eyes would cut my way, and then he'd look up at the sky or down at his feet. But he never said a word to me. Not once the whole summer.

Then, early in September, school started, and there he was, one of four new kids in the fifth grade. There are two fifth-grade classes at Henderson Elementary, and two new kids were put in each one. My class got the Trampoline Kid and Charity Jensen.

· · · · ·

On the first day I got to school early. So did a lot of other kids. And the first thing I saw when I walked into the building was a picture of me, thumbtacked to the bulletin board in the front hall. There were pictures of other kids in the school too—Sammy Malone pitching a baseball in the summer league, Rachel Jones diving into a pool, Derrick and Danny Kaminsky at a Fourth of July picnic—but my picture was the biggest. And the weirdest.

The picture had been cut out of the newspaper. It showed me high up in a huge tree, sitting on some boards tied to the branches. Two grown-ups sat behind me, both of them guys with beards. I was staring down over the edge of the platform at the photographer, with a really dumb grin on my face. The grin was because I was watching some kids messing around at the bottom of the tree—they were making me laugh at the same time that I was starting to feel sick from looking so far down.

And that just happened to be the moment when the camera clicked. The next morning, a picture of me with that dumb grin and a couple of old hippies behind me, surrounded by leaves and branches, was on the front page of the paper. I guess there wasn't much news to report that day, because the newspaper people made the picture huge—it took up almost half the front page.

Justin, my brother, said he'd seen some

idiotic looks on my face before, but that one was the best.

Adam started calling me Tree Boy. The name spread like a bad cold. I heard it at soccer day camp and from all the kids who hung out at the pool. By the time school started two weeks later, half the kids I knew were calling me Tree Boy.

Anyway, the whole thing was my mother's fault. Three days in a row she dragged me along to a place called Oriole Woods. She and fifteen or twenty other people were protesting some company's plan to cut down all the trees and build townhouses.

Lila—that's my mom's first name, and that's what I've always called her—does a lot of these protest things. I usually hate it when she makes me come along. This one wasn't so bad at first. For one thing, I really like Oriole Woods, and I didn't want the trees to get cut down. I'd played there sometimes and went on a picnic there once with Adam's family. And I thought it was cool when I'd catch a glimpse of a bright orange oriole flying around.

Some of the grown-ups built a thing to sit on and tied it up high in a tree, and people would take turns sitting up there. The tree was near the road, so whoever walked or drove by could see the protesters in the tree and down below, with their signs about protecting the woods.

The first day I actually had fun. There were a few other kids to hang around with, and I loved climbing up to the platform, even though I was a little scared the first time. I was kind of surprised that Lila even let me do it, because the branches were really high up.

It was just bad luck that the photographer came along when I was up in the tree. Because I really am a normal, average, everyday kid.

· · · · ·

That first day, when we found our new classroom, there was a strange name on the wall beside the door. A construction-paper sign said, "Grade 5—Mr. Inayatullah."

As I stared at it, two girls behind me said what I was thinking.

"I thought we were getting Ms. Wilcox." That was Deena, sounding anxious.

"Yeah, what happened to her?" Lucy said. "She was so nice."

A smiling man with brown skin and not much hair came to the door. "Ms. Wilcox transferred to another school, and I'm taking her place. I'm Mr. Inayatullah."

Mr. *What*? I thought, but none of us answered.

He seemed to read my mind. "Just call me Mr. In," he said. "Tell me your names and I'll show you where your desks and cubbies are."

I dropped my pencils and paper and ruler inside the desk, the kind with a top that lifts up. My name was printed on a card taped to the top. All the desktops were superclean, the way everything looks at the start of every school year. Then there was nothing to do but stare around at the walls—lots of maps—and the other kids coming in.

At first, I knew all the kids. I'd known most of them since kindergarten. Then, right together, in came the two newcomers.

I recognized the Trampoline Kid right away, and I thought, Cool, he's in my class. Maybe we'll be friends, and I'll get to use the trampoline. I felt pretty hopeful about that—for about a second and a half.

It's a funny thing to say about a person you've only seen on a trampoline, but this kid looked *jumpy*. He had a jerky way of walking and looking all around. He must have just had a haircut, because his white-blond hair was too short and his neck looked long and white. He was wearing the frog T-shirt.

The teacher showed him his desk—the card on it said "Brian"—and right away he sat down and stood up again. He lifted the top and closed it. Then he did it again—about five times. Every time the hinges squeaked. Finally, he sat back down, opened his backpack, and put some of his things in the desk. He shut the top and looked around. Then he got up and walked across the room, putting his hands in and out of his pockets, and about every thirty seconds he'd come back to his desk, sit down, and stand up.

Weird, I thought. My hopes of getting to use the trampoline disappeared.

The girl had freckles and long, light brown hair that was parted in the middle, perfectly straight. It hung down on each side in a tight braid. She was the only kid in the room without a backpack—she carried a red cloth bag instead. She wore a pink shirt and a blue skirt, longer than the kind most girls wear. When Mr. In went over to her and said hello, she held out her hand for a handshake. Adam and Lucy and I looked at each other with our eyebrows up and giggled. In fact, almost everybody was watching her, and almost everybody giggled. The teacher looked surprised, but he shook her hand politely and showed her where her desk was.

She didn't seem bothered by the giggling— she must have thought we were laughing at something else. She took pencils and scissors and erasers out of her bag, and spent a long time lining them up inside the desk.

The bell rang, and the principal got on the loudspeaker and welcomed everybody. Then she led us in the Pledge of Allegiance, and the speaker clattered off again. Mr. In stood in front of us with his hands in his pockets, rocking on his heels and smiling, his red tie bouncing a little against his light yellow shirt. "OK," he said. "Before we get down to serious fifth-grade learning, let's start the day by getting to know each other a bit. First—yes, Charity?"

Her hand was straight up in the air. She put it down and stood up beside her desk and said in a loud, clear voice, "Excuse me. You forgot the prayer."

Adam laughed out loud. Everybody stared.

Mr. In said, "Here, we don't pray as a group in school. However, if the class wants to have a few minutes of silence each morning for individual prayer or meditation, that would be fine with me. We can talk about that later when we set up our classroom rules."

. . . . .

When we came back from lunch, Charity stopped suddenly at the door. The Trampoline Kid was right behind her. He tripped over her and staggered into the classroom, barely managing to stay on his feet. The rest of us stepped around her. She was studying the sign that said "Grade 5—Mr. Inayatullah."

Five minutes later, when we were all looking at our new social studies books, Charity raised her hand. "Mr. Inayatullah?"

He smiled. "That's a hard name, and you got it exactly right, Charity. But it's also fine to call me Mr. In. Now, what did you want to ask?"

She smiled back at him, and I thought, show-off. In the rest of the afternoon she called him Mr. Inayatullah about five times. Every time, Adam and I rolled our eyes at each other.

Every time I rolled my eyes, it was like saying to myself, I am a normal, average, everyday kid.

. . . . .

It was warm and sunny when I headed home from school. I walked part of the way with Adam, then three more blocks after he turned off. I wanted him to come over, but he had to go to his piano lesson.

Instead of going in the front door, I went to the far end of the driveway to pet Zachary, our big old orange cat. He was lying in the grass, gazing at the five chickens scratching around in the yard behind their fence. He was probably wondering whether he could eat something that big, and when they'd come out so he could try.

We are the only people in this neighborhood who have chickens. We live right in town, where all the houses are close together and the yards are small. Keeping chickens isn't even allowed around here, and my mom got some kind of ticket from the city telling her to get rid of them. That was two months ago, but the chickens are still here. She's trying to get the city to make an exception to the rule.

I rubbed Zachary's head a few times—he loves that—and then went inside.

"Sylvan of the fifth grade!" Lila said, looking up from the computer.

"Can I have a snack?" I said.

While I ate graham crackers with peanut

butter, I told her about Mr. In and the Trampoline Kid and Charity.

"So this girl just moved here from Africa? From Kenya?" Lila said, looking really interested.

"Yeah, her whole family lived there for, like, five years. I think that's why she's so weird."

"Not weird, Sylvan. *Different.* Maybe she could tell us some interesting things about Africa."

"She's a show-off."

"Maybe she won't be such a show-off when you get to know her better."

I rolled my eyes. "I don't want to know her better."

"Well, you're going to. She's coming over for dinner tonight."

It's not unusual for us to have company for dinner. My mom likes to cook, and she likes to have people over, usually people who are involved in one of her projects. Well, she calls them projects—Will, my dad, calls them her crazy causes. So I'm used to having lots of visitors at dinnertime—but *Charity*?

"I met her mother downtown on Saturday—Dr. Jacobs works with her, and he introduced us," Lila explained. "I liked her, and they're new in town, so I thought it would be nice to have them over."

"Just wait till you meet Charity," I groaned.

. . . . .

My parents separated last spring, while I was in fourth grade. Mostly I live with Lila, but I see Will a lot on weekends and more in the summer. Justin lives with Will. That's because he's sixteen, and Lila says boys that age need to be around their fathers more. Sometimes I wish I could live there too, and hang around with Justin and Will. But then I feel bad, because that would hurt Lila's feelings. And sometimes I really do like having her all to myself.

I think Lila's projects have something to do with the divorce. Because they're what she does, most of the time. She didn't even have a job, the way most kids' moms do, until after Will left. She works part-time in a lawyer's office now, but she still spends a lot of time on things like trying to keep WalMart from opening a new store, getting people to buy fair-trade coffee, and all kinds of save-the-environment projects.

Will doesn't believe in any of that stuff. It's not that he totally disagrees with her—he cares about the environment and some of those other things too. But he doesn't see any point in all the letter writing and meetings and protests.

"I'm a practical man," he says. "I put my energy where I can actually accomplish something, like earning a living."

Will always wanted Lila to earn a living too. She had a job before I was born, but then she stayed home with me for a couple of years, and then she inherited a lot of money when her uncle died. She decided she could use that to buy groceries and stuff, and she'd put her time into making the world better instead of just trying to make money.

It sounds great when you say it like that, and when Lila talks about it, sometimes I'm really proud of her. She wants to make things better for everybody, and she's really trying to do it.

But then I remember how Will says the money she got from her uncle wasn't *that* much and that she ought to get a job and save more for college for me and Justin. And how he always had to pay more than his fair share of the bills, and anyway her crazy causes were like trying to make a river flow uphill.

So then I feel all confused, and I don't know who's right. Is Lila just being silly, trying to do something that's impossible, and not doing enough to take care of Justin and me? Or is Will being mean and not caring about other people?

Sometime I'm going to ask Justin what he thinks, if I get a chance to talk to him when Lila and Will aren't around. If he'll actually listen to me long enough.

· · · · ·

That night they came over for dinner—Charity, her mother and father, and a little sister about six or seven named Faith. We had brown rice and a stir-fry with snow peas and tofu and water chestnuts. This is one of my favorite dinners, and Charity's parents kept saying how good it was.

But Faith poked at the tofu with her fork and whined, "What is this stuff?"

"Don't be rude, Faith," Charity said. "It's good. Just eat it." She sounded exactly the way teachers sound when they're trying not to sound angry. In fact, she sounded more like a teacher than a fifth grader. It was weird.

All through dinner Lila asked a lot of questions about Kenya. Mrs. Jensen, a thin woman with a quiet, gentle voice, told us she was a nurse. She had run a clinic in a tiny village. "Martin," she said with a nod toward her husband, "was the minister in the village church."

"I'm not a minister now," Charity's father said, frowning. "I'm done with all that."

His voice was harsh, and so was the expression on his face. He was not a big man, not as big as my dad, but he looked strong. He had a lot of wild, wavy blond hair too. I would have been afraid to ask any more questions after the way he answered, but Lila wasn't.

"Oh," she said. "Was it very . . . frustrating work?"

"That's one way to put it," Mr. Jensen said. He clamped his mouth shut.

Mrs. Jensen smiled a little. "We had some difficult times toward the end of our stay. We're very glad to be back in America."

"Oh, of course," Lila said. "This country has plenty of faults, but I'm sure life is easier here. And we're glad to have you here in town."

The adults started talking about elections and stuff like that. I'd finished eating, so I got up and started to take my plate to the kitchen.

"May I please be excused?" I heard Charity say behind me. Of course Charity would have perfect manners.

"Sylvan," Lila said, "would you be a good host and show Charity and Faith the house and the garden? Maybe they'd like to see the chickens."

"OK," I mumbled. I hoped the grown-ups wouldn't spend hours talking and drinking coffee the way people usually did after dinner at our house. I didn't want to be stuck with Charity and her sister all that time.

"You want to see my room?" I said to the girls reluctantly.

They nodded and followed me up the stairs.

They stared at everything—my Star Wars figures, the Iron Man poster, my shoe boxes full of Legos. Faith poked her finger at a Stormtrooper, then at Chewbacca. "Why do boys like *ugly* dolls?" she asked Charity.

"Ask *him*," Charity answered with a shrug.

"They're not dolls," I said, annoyed. "Come on, let's go outside."

"Wait, I'd like to see these for a minute," Charity said. She reached into a box of Legos and pulled out a half-made car, then began fitting other pieces onto it.

"Haven't you ever seen Legos before?" I asked.

"I saw some the last time we visited America. But I've never played with them. I like the way they fit together."

I watched while she kept adding on to the car. When she was done, she held it up for me to see. It looked dumb—it had six wheels and two steering wheels, and she'd stacked up windows to make it really tall. "So you can stand up in it," she said, looking pleased with herself.

"Why would you want to stand up in a car?" I said. That pleased-with-herself look was bugging me.

"I don't know. For fun maybe."

"People wouldn't let you," I said. "There are laws about wearing seat belts."

"Not where Lego people live," Charity said. "They don't have car wrecks there."

How weird was that?

"Let's go outside," I said again, and this time we went.

Faith started doing cartwheels in the backyard.

"Want to see the chickens?" I asked Charity.

I like the chickens. I thought if I had to hang around with Charity, we might as well visit them.

Half of our backyard has a tall wire fence around it. Inside the fence there's one tree and a little house where the chickens go when it's cold or rainy. But it was nice out, so all five of them—two white and three red—were out scratching and pecking at the dirt and grass, which is what they do almost all the time.

"They're looking for bugs and worms to eat," I told Charity.

She gave me a look. "Everybody knows *that*." She opened the gate and went inside. I followed her. The chickens came running over to me, flapping their wings, hoping for scraps from our dinner.

"Some of our neighbors in Kenya had chickens," Charity said. "They looked different from these, though."

"The white ones are Light Brahmas. They're named Eustacia and Esmeralda," I told her. "These are Rhode Island Reds. They're the best egg layers."

Charity bent over to stroke the red-brown feathers of Zsa Zsa, the smallest hen. She's my favorite. Zsa Zsa clucked nervously and scooted away from her and toward me.

"I just hope we get to keep them," I said.

"Why wouldn't you?"

"The city says we're not supposed to have chickens. They gave my mom some kind of ticket and told her to get rid of them."

"Why do you still have them then?"

"Because my mom's trying to get the rules changed. She says people should have a right to keep animals in their yards as long as the animals aren't bothering anybody."

By now Zsa Zsa had figured out that I wasn't carrying food, but she still kept pecking around my sneakers. She does that a lot. I guess it means she likes me.

"Where do you live, anyway?" I asked.

"Bradley Street."

"That's not very far from here."

"I know. That's why we walked over instead of driving."

"Does anybody on your street have chickens?" I asked.

"I don't think so. I haven't seen any."

Faith had stopped cartwheeling and come into the chickens' pen. She was chasing Esmeralda, who was getting really upset. She'd dash halfway across the yard, then look back and see Faith scrambling after her, and then dash off again, flapping and clucking.

"Hey, cut it out!" I yelled at Faith. "Stop chasing her."

"Look, they're getting out," Charity said.

I turned and saw that Faith had left the gate open. Drucilla and Eustacia were waddling down the driveway toward the street, with Zsa Zsa close behind them.

I ran like mad, trying to get past them and shoo them back. But the noise I made spooked them. The chickens fluttered up a few feet in the air and came down running. At the end of the driveway Eustacia hustled off to the left, Drucilla dashed right, and Zsa Zsa headed straight for the street.

I saw the front of a car, heard brakes squeal, and everything stopped. There was Zsa Zsa, unhurt, standing right in front of the car. I grabbed her and held her tight. A man with a pointy nose and tiny glasses poked his head out the car window and said, "Is that a *chicken*?"

My heart was still pounding so hard, all I could do was nod and keep breathing. I backed away from the street. The car moved on. Lila, who'd heard the squeal, rushed out the front door and shooed Drucilla and Eustacia back to their pen. Luckily Charity had closed the gate in time to keep Esmeralda and Josephine in. She and Faith were still inside too. Faith looked wide-eyed. I had a feeling Charity had already chewed her out for leaving the gate open.

"Faith," Charity said as we finally got all the chickens into the pen, "I hope you have learned your lesson."

chapter two

CHARITY

He had been very high up in the air, against the hot blue sky of Kenya where birds dipped and circled. And then he fell—dropped hard and crumpled against the ground. Before the crowd closed around him, I saw him for just a moment. That glimpse was like a photograph that my mind took and kept, even though I did not want to keep it.

He lay on his side, with his legs apart and one foot turned at an angle that seemed wrong.

The foot twitched for a moment. One arm was stuck under him, and his other hand lay near his chin. The hand also twitched, once. Unless it was my own shudder that made it seem that it twitched. Because his head was twisted back—just slightly, but it wasn't right. A head doesn't turn that way. I saw the white part of the eyes in his wrinkled face, but I couldn't see the dark part that should have been in the middle, the center of the eyes that had so often given me their gentle, strange look.

He was Mr. Kafuna, my father's assistant, the caretaker of the church. I had known him as long as we'd lived in Africa. I knew one of his daughters. I knew four of his grandchildren. And if it weren't for my father, he would still be alive.

· · · · ·

"Aren't we—aren't we going to say grace?" I said, looking at my father.

Our food was on the table—a big platter of cornmeal *ugali*, a bowl of chicken in some kind of sauce, and a smaller bowl of the greens that people call *sukuma wiki*. The table was set as usual, with forks and spoons and shiny blue tin plates and tin cups filled with water. It was almost dark out, so the kerosene lamp overhead was burning with its usual soft whooshing sound. The four of us were sitting there as usual too—my mother and father; my little sister, Faith; and me.

We were all staring at my father.

My father is the kind of person that people notice. He's not very tall, but he's solid and strong, with a face that looks strong too. And he has long blond hair that's always wild and rumpled. Bwana Simba—that was what some people called him. It means Mr. Lion. Some of them gave a sly laugh when they said it. But they didn't call him that to his face.

But of course, that's the way Dad always looks. We weren't staring at him because of his strong face or his wild hair. We were staring because all the plates were still empty except his, and he was forking in big mouthfuls of *ugali* and chicken and chewing them up like a machine.

In my entire life, I had never seen Dad start a meal without saying grace.

The wordless staring went on for a very long minute or two. The only sounds were the clicks of Dad's fork against the plate, the chatter of insects, and the rumble of faraway drums. Dad wasn't looking at any of us. His eyes seemed to be fixed on the open window and the shadowy field of sugarcane beyond it. Mom opened her mouth and shut it again, with her hands gripping the table edge on either side of her plate. Faith squirmed in her chair, but her eyes stayed on Dad as if she was a snake and he was the snake charmer's flute.

So it was up to me, and I said it: "Aren't we going to say grace?"

I was trying to sound totally normal, but even I could hear the nervousness in my voice.

My father laid down his fork and looked around at all three of us before resting his gaze on me. "No, Charity," he said, "we are not going to say grace." His voice was as flat as the bottom of a frying pan. "We are not going to say grace in this house again."

Three weeks later we moved to America.

. . . . .

On a baking-hot August day, Mom drove me to our new house, following the borrowed pickup truck that held Dad and Faith and almost everything we owned.

"Here's our street," Mom said, as the truck turned onto a narrow street lined with big trees and old houses with small, neat yards. Mom sounded cheerful. I knew she was happy to be moving out of Grandpa and Grandma's house, where we'd been for the last few weeks, and into our own place.

It was a green wooden house with a pointed roof, not very wide but two stories tall. The front porch held a swing big enough for two or three people. We looked at a lot of different houses before Mom and Dad bought this one. There was a blue house that I liked better, but Faith wanted this one because of the swing.

"Did you really buy this house because Faith wanted the swing?" I asked Mom.

She laughed. "Not hardly. We bought it because it was the best house in our price range. It's in good shape, it's near the school, and it's in a safe neighborhood. But the swing is a nice touch."

The pickup truck pulled into the driveway beside the house, and Mom parked on the street. Right away Faith ran up the steps and sat in the swing. For a second I thought I should be really grown up and start carrying boxes. But then I ran to the swing too and jumped in beside her. My legs were long enough to push off and get us moving. For a few minutes we sat there, giggling and swinging in the cool breeze.

Mom smiled at us and picked up a box from the back of the truck, but Dad said, "Lend a hand, girls. You can get some of the smaller boxes."

Dad had been glad to get out of Grandma and Grandpa's house too, but he was never completely happy about anything, not since we left Kenya.

Mom said our new house was smaller than Grandma and Grandpa's, but it didn't seem like it when we walked in. It seemed huge, probably because it was totally empty—just white walls and scuffed wooden floors and bare windows. Faith and I ran around exploring everything.

We found Mom standing in the middle of the kitchen, looking around. "A real kitchen," she said softly.

We had just finished unloading all our things when the doorbell rang. Four musical notes echoed through the empty house. At the first note we all jumped slightly, startled. Grandpa and Grandma had a doorbell too, but it just rang one note. Faith lit up like she'd heard the angels singing.

"Visitors already?" Mom said, heading for the door, but Faith raced ahead of her. There was a girl about my age standing there, a girl with curly dark brown hair.

"How did you do that?" Faith said, bobbing up and down on her toes.

The girl stared at her. "Do what?"

"Make that sound," she said impatiently.

"Don't be silly, Faith," I said. "It's a doorbell, just like Grandma's." The girl's mouth was hanging open slightly.

"But it *sings*," Faith said.

The girl pointed to something on the outside of the house, and Faith went out and started pushing the button over and over.

"Hello," Mom called out over the ringing. "We're the Jensens. Do you live nearby?"

"Yeah, over there," the girl said, pointing to her right. She was still recovering from the shock of meeting Faith. "My name's Lucy."

"That's Faith, and this is Charity," Mom said. "Would you like to come in?"

"OK," Lucy said.

Right then Dad came scowling out of the kitchen, where he'd just set down a big box of cooking pots and dishes. *Ding, ding-dong, dong* echoed for about the fifteenth time. "Faith!" Dad boomed, and there was no more dinging and donging.

Lucy stared up at Dad and started to tug at a curl just above her ear.

"Martin," Mom said. "This is Lucy. She lives down the street."

"Hi, Lucy." Then he looked at the pile of

boxes on the floor and said, "Well, let's get these things put away."

The biggest things we had were the table, which leaned against a wall, waiting for its legs to be screwed back on, and Mom and Dad's mattress, which we had pushed into the room that was going to be their bedroom. Four folding chairs leaned against the wall next to the table. That left only the boxes, each labeled with a name—Debbie, Martin, Charity, Faith—or "kitchen" or "bathroom."

"Do you want to see my room?" I asked Lucy. Even though being in America felt like I'd moved to a different planet, I was excited about having a room to myself.

Lucy and I each picked up a box labeled "Charity," and I led the way upstairs to my room, which I'd seen only once before, when Mom and Dad were deciding whether to buy the house. Earlier, in between carrying boxes in from the truck, I'd darted in once to make sure it was still there.

It had a window covered with a torn roll-up shade and a dusty closet where some wire coat hangers dangled. I put my box down and opened the shade. The nearest window of the house next door was full of potted plants.

Lucy set down her box in the middle of the floor and looked around. "It's your own room?" she asked. "You don't have to share it?"

"Yes, it's all mine."

"Awesome," she sighed. "I have to share a room with my big sister. She talks in her sleep and wakes me up."

"Well, I used to have to share with Faith, and she always woke me up too early in the morning. This is the first time I've had my own room."

"Are you ten?"

I nodded. "Are you?"

"I'll be eleven in October."

We went down to the front room and picked up two more boxes—my clothes and my books. The pile seemed much smaller. Lucy glanced around. "When's the moving van coming?"

"The what?"

"The moving van. With all your furniture and stuff."

"Oh." For a second I didn't know what to say. I hadn't been inside many American houses, but from Grandma and Grandpa's house, and what I'd seen on their TV, I had some idea of how many things Americans could own. Our house must have looked pretty empty to Lucy. "Well, we don't actually have any furniture. I mean, we're going to get beds," I added quickly.

I explained about how we'd just moved here from Kenya, so we couldn't bring much with us on the plane. I decided not to say just yet that in Kenya we didn't have very much anyway. A table and chairs, two beds, a small sofa.

"Kenya?" Lucy asked. "Where's that?"

"It's in Africa. East Africa."

"What were you doing there? How long were you there?"

In the month we'd spent at Grandma and Grandpa's house, right after we arrived in America, I'd answered the same questions about fifty times, from all of Grandma and Grandpa's friends and neighbors. So I gave Lucy the short and simple answers.

"My mom and dad were missionaries. My dad was a pastor and my mom was a nurse, in a little village. We were there almost five years."

"Wow, no wonder your sister doesn't know about doorbells."

"Faith doesn't know *anything*. She's only six."

We took the last "Charity" boxes into my room. Mom poked her head in and said, "Dad's taking the truck back, and I'm following him in the car so I can bring him back here. We should be back in thirty or forty minutes. You girls be good, and don't wander off, all right?"

"Don't *worry*," I said, with a loud, dramatic sigh. "I'm not going to get lost."

Mom ignored this. "Look after Faith," she said sternly.

"Tell her she has to listen to me."

"I already did," Mom answered and headed out the front door.

Lucy and I walked around the house, poking into closets and kitchen cabinets, but there wasn't much to see. Faith's room was smaller than mine, and she'd already put her clothes away. Under her window she'd spread out one of Grandma and Grandpa's blankets. The blankets were what Faith and I had to sleep on until we got our beds. She was sitting on the floor, taking her dolls out of a box, and didn't even look up when we stood for a minute in the doorway.

"Do you want to go outside?" I said.

We went out the front door, and Lucy pointed out her house, two doors down the street. Most of the houses were right next to the sidewalk, with no front yards, just a few shrubs. We walked down the driveway and into our small backyard, which was surrounded by a wooden fence that came up to my shoulder.

There was one big tree in the back left corner of the yard and a few scraggly plants along the fence. It was warm and muggy, and the grass looked dry. I reminded myself that this was upstate New York, and it would get cold here eventually—really cold. But right then it felt a lot like Kenya, even though it looked completely different.

It was a good thing we came back to America in the summer, because we'd have some time to get the coats and boots and blankets we hadn't needed in Africa. For a moment I remembered snow and sledding and making snowmen and feeling icy flakes land on your tongue. It would be nice to see snow again.

When I was little, Mom would take me sledding at the church where Dad was the pastor. Our own yard was perfectly flat, but the church was on a little hill, and Mom would put me on the plastic sled and give me a push, and I'd go sailing down. And the thought of sledding reminded me of the church itself, the smooth wooden pews and thick red carpet, and how the light came through the stained glass window that showed Jesus with the loaves and fishes.

While we were still at Grandma and Grandpa's house, I asked Mom and Dad when we would find a church to go to, because our old church was in a different town and I knew it was too far to go every Sunday. Mom said we'd find one soon, once we were settled in our new house. Dad didn't say anything.

Lucy found a small greenish ball in the grass

and started tossing it in the air and catching it.

"What church do you go to?" I asked her.

"I don't go to church," she answered, tossing the ball again.

My mouth dropped open. "You don't?"

She caught the ball and looked at me with a shrug.

"You mean your parents don't take you? Your whole family never goes?" My whole life, I thought every nice, decent person went to church. It was as normal as brushing your teeth.

"We just don't go," Lucy said. "Lots of people don't go."

"*Nice* people go," I said.

The ball bounced out of Lucy's hands. "Well, thanks a lot."

"I didn't mean—" But she had already turned around and was marching off down the driveway.

I really hadn't meant to insult her. But as her back disappeared, I shrugged. Her family must be kind of strange, I thought. Probably I wouldn't be allowed to play with her anyway.

I went back inside. In my new room, I opened

each of my boxes and put the clothes in the closet. I folded in the top flaps of two boxes, where I was keeping my books and other things. Soon I'd have my own bed. In Kenya I'd shared one with Faith, and that was the only furniture in our room.

. . . . .

That night I lay on two folded blankets and stared out the moonlit window. The blankets didn't do much to cushion the floor. I could hear Mom talking softly to Faith in the next room, probably rubbing her back, trying to get her to sleep. I wasn't sure I could sleep either. It was all so strange.

At Grandma and Grandpa's, Mom and Dad had had the guest room. Faith and I slept on the same couch, heads at opposite ends, kicking each other all night. Grandma and Grandpa's house was cluttered with all kinds of odd things—pictures covered the walls, a collection of ceramic roosters stood on top of the kitchen cabinets, and books and jars of seashells and fake flowers lined the shelves.

People came and went all the time, cousins and aunts and uncles and neighbors, all curious to see us. We'd visited only three or four times since we'd moved to Kenya, and everyone said how big Faith and I had grown. Were they expecting us to shrink? Everyone was nice, but sometimes I felt like an exhibit in a zoo.

Now all that commotion was over, and I was lying on the floor in a quiet, bare house. I'd already said my prayers. Faith must have fallen asleep, because the sounds from her room had stopped. Very faintly, I could hear our parents moving around, farther down the hall.

This house felt so empty. The whole neighborhood felt empty. I'd met one girl my age, but she was strange and went away angry. Or maybe I was the one who was strange.

I remembered running all around the sugarcane and cornfields with Grace and Esther and Lydia and Grace's little brothers, Daniel and Peter. Grace's mother helped us make dolls out of rags, and Lydia's older brother could make amazing toys out of pieces of wire. All those kids were my friends, and being with them was easy, even though I looked different from them. But in this new place I didn't know anyone, and I had a feeling that no one I'd meet here would understand my old life.

Our house in Kenya had been made of concrete blocks painted bright green and blue, with a roof of wavy sheets of metal that sounded like thunder whenever it rained. The bedrooms had curtains instead of doors. We didn't have much there, but it seemed like enough.

This place felt hollow as a gourd. I didn't know if we could fill it. It would be hardest for Dad and me, I thought. Mom and Faith would do all right here—Mom had her nursing job at the hospital, and Faith was little and excited about everything new. But Dad didn't seem to know what to do now that he wasn't a pastor anymore, and I felt so alone. I couldn't see how either of us was going to live here.

chapter three

SYLVAN

Right after Will moved out last February, I was mad all the time. It felt like there was a big hole in my life. After the first couple of days, he called and said he'd come by to pick up me and Justin on Saturday morning so we could spend some time together. When he came to get us, Lila stayed in the kitchen, and Will didn't come inside. He just knocked on the door like a stranger, and Justin and I got our jackets and went outside. He hugged us both hard and said he was sorry. And I couldn't say a single word. Because

I loved the feel and smell of him hugging me—
it was like pure cold water after being thirsty a
long time—but that didn't stop me from being
angry deep down.

Will was staying with a friend of his. For
about a month, even though he sometimes
called me or took me and Justin to get pizza or
see a movie, there wasn't any regular time that
I could count on being with him. Home was all
wrong without him there. Everything felt dark
and empty.

Justin was silent and sometimes he was mean,
and he stayed out really late with his friends, even
on school nights. Lila was all upset and cried a lot,
and even though she gave me hugs and told me
things would get better, I wasn't sure I believed
her. She stopped doing work for her projects and
never made me or Justin do anything. She didn't
check if I'd done my homework. She didn't even
try to make Justin come home on time or pick up
the clothes he left lying around. My school chorus
had a concert, and Lila came, but Will didn't and
neither did Justin.

I got in a lot of trouble at school. I failed tests because I didn't study and didn't even try very hard when the test paper was in front of me. I'd always gotten along OK with our teacher, Mr. Fitzpatrick, but suddenly I hated him. Who did he think he was, trying to be Mr. Nice Guy, always patting us on the shoulder and asking what's new and talking to all the boys about baseball? It was all fake, I told myself.

Then in April there was another bad thing, at least for me—Justin moved into Will's apartment. It felt like I'd never again have Justin kidding around with me, giving me big-brother advice, pretending to trip me when I walked past him and telling Lila to give me a break. I wouldn't say good-bye to him, and after he was gone, I lay on my bed and cried.

But after that, things settled down more. We got into a regular pattern—I stayed with Lila on school nights and with Will and Justin on the weekends. Some days after school, instead of taking the bus to Will's apartment, Justin walked to Lila's and hung around with us for a while. Will picked him up after he finished work.

Lila started acting more normal. She didn't get upset as often, and she went back to working on her causes. She made big pots of soup and loaves of bread and apple pies, and people came over for dinner again. She said she needed to earn money for herself and got a job in a lawyer's office, part-time so she could be home when I got out of school.

I didn't feel as bad as before, but I was still getting in trouble at school.

· · · · ·

The worst day at school was a Thursday about three weeks before the end of the year. That morning Lila was in a really bad mood. I think she might have been talking to Will on the phone while I was in the shower. She snapped at me about leaving my cereal bowl on the table, about not putting away my clean clothes like she'd told me to the night before, about practically everything.

So I went to school in a bad mood too. And when things started to go wrong there, I just wasn't ready to handle even the tiniest problem. I was ready to flip out. And that's what I did.

. . . . .

The first disaster came when Mr. Fitzpatrick handed back the math quiz from the day before. There was a big red 45 at the top of mine. I caught my breath. Math was always hard for me, and this time I hadn't even bothered to study. Still, I'd never gotten a grade that low in *anything*.

But the shock in my insides turned into something stony hard. So what? I hate math anyway.

Mr. Fitzpatrick finished handing out the papers and spoke from the front of the room. "Most of you did quite well on this quiz—congratulations," he said. "But I want to make sure everyone really knows this material. So for tomorrow, please correct everything you got wrong. If you don't understand how to do it, you can ask me during free time this afternoon."

He turned to write a new assignment on the board, and slowly I began to crumple the quiz paper in my hands. Mr. Fitzpatrick must have heard the noise, but he didn't turn around. All the kids were watching me, and I played it up. I squeezed the paper until it was nothing but a little wad in my fist.

Mr. Fitzpatrick put down the chalk and began explaining what he'd written, but I wasn't listening. I just stared at my hands. They were shifting the wad of paper back and forth, back and forth, from one hand to the other.

Then I felt something near me and looked up. Mr. Fitzpatrick was standing right next to my desk, looking grim. "Sylvan," he said slowly, "is that your math quiz?"

I stared at the wad and nodded.

"Aren't you going to need that paper so you can correct it?"

I nodded again.

"Take it home this afternoon and flatten it out," he ordered. "Tomorrow I want to see every single problem done correctly."

My eyes were still on the crumpled paper, and this time I didn't even nod. I just clenched my teeth. I'd never be able to read the quiz now.

I couldn't do the math problems anyway. And I wasn't going to try.

I decided I wouldn't ask for Mr. Fitzpatrick's help during free time. But it didn't matter anyway, because for me, free time never came. Soon after the terrible math paper we went out for recess. And that was when I really got in trouble.

I stalked around the playground, kicking rocks and hating Will and Lila and Justin and Mr. Fitzpatrick and anybody else I could think of. But then Adam ran over to me and said, "Come on, we're gonna play soccer and we need you." And since I really felt like kicking something, I decided to play.

There was just one problem with playing soccer with the kids in my fourth-grade class, and the name of that problem was Leo. He was the biggest kid in the class, and even though he wasn't that great at controlling the ball or scoring, he was very good at shoving people out of the way and "accidentally" kicking your shin instead of the ball. So anytime a few kids were scrambling to get the ball, Leo usually came with it. And somebody might yell "foul," but we didn't have real referees. Even if a teacher was watching, when a knot of kids are struggling for the ball, the teacher can't tell whether someone's ankle got kicked by accident or not.

So Leo got away with bruising a lot of people's legs. But not that day.

Adam and I were on the same team, and we're both pretty good, but the other team had Peter, who is just as good or maybe better. They also had Leo. But I wasn't playing very well—probably because I was in such a bad mood—and the other team took a 3–1 lead. Then they nailed two goals, one right after the other, and one of them I definitely should have stopped.

"Sylvan," Adam groaned.

"What?" I snapped back.

"Never mind, 's OK," he called. "Come on, let's get 'em!"

I threw myself back into the game. Nothing was going to get by me now. And right away I found myself up against big Leo.

Adam tried to pass to Eli, but Adam's kick

was off target, and Leo and I both rushed after the ball. We got to it at the same time. I got a toe on it, but Leo leaned into me, forcing me to step back. But before he could kick the ball clear, I snaked my foot around his, pulling the ball toward me. That's when I got a slammer of a kick in the back of my right leg. My right knee crumpled to the ground, but I was up in a second and boiling over.

"You—!" Well, I'd better not repeat what I said.

Leo wasn't used to people fighting back. Ignoring me, he moved up to kick the ball.

After that, it was like my right arm had a mind of its own. I didn't mean to do anything, I swear. But my fist swung out like a hammer and smacked against the side of Leo's head, and big Leo actually fell to the ground. I felt a half second of surprise, but it didn't stop the boiling inside me. I kicked his shins about five times as he lay on the ground before Mr. Fitzpatrick pulled me off.

The whole class stared as he gripped my arm and marched me to the principal's office. I got scared, even though I was still mad. The principal, Ms. Langley, was sometimes nice and sometimes mean. Kids who got in trouble never knew if she was going to let them off easy or give them every punishment she could think of. Once Kyle and I were just shoving each other a little, and she started yelling about how both of us were going to end up in jail someday.

I guess she was in an OK mood this time, because she didn't yell. She gave me a lecture, phoned Lila, and sent me home with a two-day suspension. And I had to write a letter apologizing to Leo.

I'd already been in a couple of other fights that spring. But after this one, something changed. Kids gave me funny looks. In the halls, when smaller kids saw me, they got out of my way really fast. Once I heard a girl say she was scared of me.

Nobody wanted to make me mad, and that was fine with me. But I didn't feel too good about my new reputation. Kids didn't seem to like me as much as they used to. Mr. Fitzpatrick looked suspicious whenever I asked to go to the bathroom or the library. If other teachers saw me alone in the hall, they looked suspicious too. And Lila was always asking me questions about school, my friends, how I was feeling.

By the end of fourth grade, I still felt angry a lot, but more than anything I wanted to erase the past few months and just be a normal, average, everyday kid.

· · · · ·

On the first Friday of fifth grade, I got home a little after three. As usual, Adam and I had a plan. We were both going to ask our moms if we could hang out at his house, and then I'd call him to let him know.

I hurried up our front steps and yanked on the door, but it was locked. This happened sometimes when Lila had to go somewhere, and she always left the back door unlocked for me. Justin had his own key, but he wouldn't be home for another half hour. I ran around to the back, and it was open. Dropping my backpack just inside the door, I went to the kitchen, where Lila always left notes for me beside the toaster.

Usually her notes said things like "Getting groceries—back by 3:30" or "meeting at Doug's house, see you around 4:00." But this note was different. It said, "Hi Sylvan. Please get a snack if you want, and then walk downtown and meet me near the big clock. There's something going on that I want you to be part of. Love, Lila."

"Awww," I groaned. Whatever the "something going on" was, I'd rather have gone to Adam's. I didn't have a choice, though. I called Adam and told him I couldn't come, grabbed a handful of peanuts from a jar, and walked downtown.

It wasn't far, maybe five or six blocks. The big clock stood on a corner of the Commons, a block that used to be a street but now is just a brick place for people to walk between the stores.

When I got there, I wanted to turn around and run home.

Because it wasn't just Lila hanging around near the clock. There were about twelve or fifteen people there, in a ragged line facing the street at the end of the Commons. They were holding up big signs so the drivers could read them.

I should have known it was something like this, I thought.

The people's backs were toward me, so I couldn't see the signs. But I could easily spot Lila's long brown-and-gray hair, hanging down her back against her favorite dark purple T-shirt. And I could hear her voice among the voices chanting, "Save the deer! Save the deer!"

I am not a shouting-on-the-street-corner kind of person. And I knew what Lila wanted me there for—she wanted me to hold a sign and yell with the rest of them.

It had been a while since she'd made me do something like that. The candlelight vigils—for peace or for death-row prisoners or for AIDS victims—weren't so bad. At least it was dark. But in the daytime, standing out where everybody in the entire town could see you, holding a big sign and yelling? That was horrible. She couldn't make me yell, but she made me hold a sign a couple of times, like at the protest against Walmart a couple years ago.

She didn't make Justin do stuff like this. He told her he wouldn't, and she let him get away with it, just because he's a teenager.

I had told her this stuff was totally embarrassing. I told her I hated doing it. But she said there was nothing to be embarrassed about—we were getting people's attention for a good cause.

But all the grown-ups were doing it because they wanted to. The kids didn't have a choice.

And Walmart got built anyway.

Staring at the protest group, I thought about walking back home or back to Adam's house. I could say I never saw the note, I thought. I could say I tried to call her from Adam's, but no one was home.

The trouble was that Lila had an iron rule: I always had to come straight home and check in first. And anyway, she'd be worried about me if I didn't show up at the protest, and then she'd be angry no matter what excuse I thought up.

I stood there as long as I dared. I stood there

so long a turtle could have made it from school to the Commons. And then I went. Dragging my feet, I walked over to the group.

"Hey, Sylvan!" Lila was beaming. "Pick up a sign. There's a few over there." She pointed to a stack of them leaning against a bench.

I squeezed my fists in the pockets of my shorts. "I'm tired," I said in my tired, whiny voice. "Can't I just sit on the bench and watch?"

She shook her head. "Grab a sign. You need to be part of this."

"Why?" I said in my grumpy voice.

"Because the county has a crazy plan to kill all the deer they can find, just because some of them are coming into people's yards and eating their plants. There are perfectly good ways to keep the deer out without shooting them."

That kind of made sense, but it didn't make standing on the sidewalk with a sign any less embarrassing. I argued some more, but after a while I picked out the smallest sign—it said "No Killing"—and joined the group.

Lila's friends Doug and Marietta were

there, along with their two kids, a girl and a boy who are too little to mind getting dragged along. The boy is in kindergarten, and he kept jumping around and dropping his sign. The girl was practically a baby. She just sat in a stroller with a sign attached to it that said "Don't hurt Bambi."

Doug is kind of wide, and I stood behind him until Lila pushed me to the front.

I tried not to look at the people driving or walking by. If anybody I knew was going to see me in the crowd, I didn't want to know about it. I kept my face in an expression that (I hoped) said, "I'm only doing this because they're making me," and I kept my eyes on the ground.

But that got boring fast, so I watched the other people in the group. Nobody else had a "they're making me do this" expression. Most of them looked happy—I guess they liked holding signs and shouting and being stared at. Lila looked like the happiest one of all. She was smiling and pumping her sign up and down, full of energy.

Just then I spotted two kids from my class, Kyle and James, crossing the street and heading right toward us. I tried to sneak behind Doug again, but they saw me anyway.

"Tree Boy!" Kyle yelled. "Hey, Tree Boy, where's your tree?"

Kyle wears black T-shirts and camouflage pants almost every day, and he always acts really tough. He thinks he's a soldier or something. I never liked him all that much, and at that moment I hated him.

"Ha-ha," I said sarcastically. I still held the sign in one hand, but it was dragging on the ground.

"I didn't know you were one of the hippies, dude," James said, looking around at the group. James is Kyle's best friend. He has glasses and wears camo shirts, not camo pants. So he and Kyle always match, sort of.

"I'm not," I said. "My mom makes me do this, OK?"

"Sure he's a hippie," Kyle said. "Didn't he look like one up in the tree? They do this stuff for fun."

"Weird," James said.

I wanted to feel my fist slam into Kyle's head and James's too, just the way it slammed into Leo's. I dropped the sign, but I forced my hands not to clench into fists.

James took a step back. "Come on, Kyle, let's get going."

"Yeah, get going," I muttered.

"Have fun, Tree Boy," Kyle said, and they walked away, shuffling toward the store with all the comic books and games.

I am *not* a hippie, I thought. I hate holding signs. And I did not beat up Kyle and James even though they deserve it.

I stood there with the sign at my feet and my back to the group, watching all the lucky people strolling in the sunshine, looking in store windows and sitting around on benches. All doing whatever they wanted to do. And then I saw Justin and a friend of his, walking along with skateboards tucked under their arms. You weren't allowed to skate on the Commons, but there was a skate park a few blocks away. That had to be where they were headed.

I stepped on the sign and hurried over to him. "Hey, Justin!"

He stopped. "Hey, little bro."

"Can I come with you?"

He and his friend looked at each other.

"Come with me where?" Justin said in a slow, drawly voice. "Where am I going?"

"To the skate park?" I said eagerly.

"Um, are we going to the skate park?" he asked his friend.

The other boy shook his head. "I don't know, dude. I don't know where we're going."

I was bouncing on my toes. "Come on, Justin. Let me go with you."

"Naah. No can do."

I glanced back to see if Lila was coming to get me, but she wasn't, not yet anyway. "Please, Justin? Look what she's making me do."

"All you're doing is talking to us," he said with a shrug.

"She's making me hold up a sign. She makes

me stand in front of everybody right beside the street where everybody stares at us. It's totally embarrassing."

He glanced over at the protest group, and for a second I thought he might give in. Then he shook his head. "We've got things to do—we're not just gonna be hanging at the skate park. Can't take you this time." He turned to his friend. "Let's move."

"Justin!" I wailed to his back.

He actually did turn around. "Look, Sylvan, I know it sucks," he said quietly. "But they'll wind down pretty soon and you'll get to go home. And it's Friday, remember? Will's gonna pick you up as soon as he's done with work, OK?"

"OK," I mumbled, and he walked away.

I watched their backs going away, and then I looked at the group again. Lila was hurrying toward me. "What are you doing?" she called. "Come back and get your sign."

And very, very, very, slowly, I did.

chapter four

CHARITY

From the start, I couldn't understand my new school. I didn't know what I was supposed to do half the time.

For one thing, no one in the school ever said a prayer. It was like there was something wrong with praying. Also, they didn't stand up when the teacher called on them. We always had to do that at my old school. On my first day at the new school, I stood up whenever I spoke to the teacher. By the end of the day, though, I saw that no one else did. They would stare at me for it too.

They all looked at me with such cold faces, as if I wasn't like them at all. Even Lucy, who I'd met, acted as if she'd never seen me before.

That evening Mom and Dad and Faith and I went to Sylvan's house for dinner. When Mom told me we were going, she said there was a boy about my age, but I was surprised when he turned out to be in my same class. I didn't know his name, but I remembered seeing his face—kind of thin, with big brown eyes and dark brown hair.

Sylvan's mother was nice, and she listened to everything Mom and I told her about Kenya. Then Sylvan's mother and my dad started talking about politics and things like that, so I wanted to go somewhere else.

Sylvan wasn't especially friendly, but at least he showed us his room and his yard and the chickens. Then Faith went and let the chickens out. There was a lot of running around and yelling, and one of the chickens almost got hit by a car. I had to explain to Faith very clearly what can happen when you leave a gate open.

As the four of us walked home from Sylvan's house that night, I felt tired and a little sad. I hoped I'd find a real friend soon. It wasn't going to be Lucy. It wasn't going to be Sylvan, who was maybe all right, but after all he was a boy. And besides, he called his mother by her first name, Lila, instead of Mom or Mother. I'd never heard of anybody doing that before. It didn't seem right.

· · · · ·

At the start of the second day of school, when I went in the classroom and shook Mr. Inayatullah's hand, he gave me a big smile. I think he likes me, and I like him. He doesn't act as if there's anything wrong with me.

But when I turned toward my seat, Lucy and the girl next to her, Natasha, were giggling, and they were looking at me. I quickly sat down at my desk and kept my eyes away from them.

Why did they laugh? Was it my clothes—the blue skirt from my old school uniform? I knew my clothes were plain compared to all the different things kids wore at this school. At my old school I hardly ever thought about clothes. We all wore the same thing—dark blue skirts for girls, dark blue shorts for boys, and light blue shirts for everybody. None of us owned very many other clothes. Some of the kids didn't have *any* other clothes, except a couple of old worn-out things.

On the third day, I arrived at the same time as Adam, who is probably the loudest boy in the class, and two other boys named Peter and Eli. I shook Mr. Inayatullah's hand and said, "Good morning."

Right beside me, I heard a little snort from Adam. "Hey, Charity," he said. "How come you shake his hand every day?"

He was grinning as if I'd done something really funny. That's when I realized that not one of the three boys had shaken the teacher's hand. Peter and Eli were staring at me too. My heart sank. Another thing I thought was normal turned out not to be normal in America.

"I'm sure that's what everyone did in your school in Kenya, right, Charity?" Mr. Inayatullah said.

I nodded gratefully.

"In some cultures, Adam," he went on, smiling, "students are expected to greet their teachers politely every day, with a handshake and a 'good morning.' Not a bad idea, in my opinion. I wouldn't mind seeing a little more politeness"—his eyebrows arched up at Adam—"from certain students."

"Oh—yeah" was all Adam said, but he looked uncomfortable, and he quickly went to put his backpack away.

Mr. Inayatullah looked thoughtfully at me. "I think in one of our morning meetings it would be a good idea if you told the whole class about a typical day in your old school—what you did each morning, what you studied, and what your school looked like. I'd be very interested to hear about it myself."

"All—all right," I said.

"How about Tuesday? That will give you a little time to think about what you want to say."

. . . . .

On Tuesday, at morning meeting time, the whole class sat in a circle on a big blue rug in the corner of the room. Mr. In sat on the floor too. That day, like every other day, he was wearing blue jeans and a red tie. His shirt might be white or yellow or blue, and his tie might have stripes or dots or penguins on it, but the tie was always mostly red.

A few students were whispering and elbowing one another, but most of them were just looking at me. I passed around some pictures my mom had taken of the school, me and my friends in our school uniforms, the marketplace, and the clinic. I was nervous. Even though I'd thought a lot about the kinds of things I would tell them, I suddenly had no idea how to start.

I looked at all the faces staring at me, then at Mr. Inayatullah. I think he knew how I felt, because he said, "Why don't you begin by telling us about a typical day at school? What did you do first thing in the morning?"

So I told them how each day began.

· · · · ·

Mornings were cool, with dew on the grass where everyone gathered. The teachers stood in front of the flagpole, and each class stood together, the prefects ordering everybody into rows. We all looked alike in our blue uniforms, except that some kids wore sweaters over theirs. And except that Faith and I always stood out, because we were the only white kids in the school.

The headmistress would make announcements, the religious knowledge teacher would say a prayer, and then we'd all sing the Kenyan national anthem. It's in Swahili, and it's very beautiful.

We'd draw out the last note, so it would linger softly in the air. Then everyone would shout "Nyayo!" which means something like following in the footprints of the leaders. Instantly the neat rows would break up, everybody jostling and chattering, and we'd all go inside to our classes.

The school had two buildings, each with a row of classrooms that weren't connected to one another by any doors or halls. You had to go outside to move from one room to another. Inside, there weren't any computers. There weren't even electric lights. Most of the other schools in Kenya had electricity, but Shibuye Primary School was too small and too far from any town.

Each desk was made for two kids, who sat on a single bench without a back. I shared a desk with my best friend, Grace Mbaya. Grace was a skinny girl who liked to laugh more than anybody I ever met. At break time or after school she'd try to braid my hair into little rows the way the African girls did theirs. A lot of times, girls would sit around in the yard outside the school, talking and doing one another's hair. It didn't really work with my hair because it's so straight. And that would make her giggle.

One time Grace let me try to make rows in her hair, with another girl telling me what to do, but my fingers were clumsy, and when she looked in the mirror, she laughed again. "Aiee!" she said. "A rat makes a nest in my hair!" All the other girls laughed too, but I didn't mind. They weren't laughing to be mean. A *mzungu*—white person—wasn't supposed to know how to plait hair. Besides, they all thought my hair was special because it was so different from theirs.

Sometimes I would read stories out loud to Grace, because I could read English a lot better than she could. We both liked stories. Her house didn't have many books, so usually we read at my house. And Grace taught me some Luhya, the language she and her family spoke at home. The first time I said, "Good morning. How are you?" in Luhya to Grace's mother, she threw up her hands and laughed exactly like Grace.

I was puzzled and a little hurt, because I was proud of the new words I'd learned. "Did I say it wrong?" I asked Grace.

"No," said Grace. "You speak our language very well. She is just happy." Then she grinned and added in a teasing voice, "You are speaking Luhya like a *mzungu*."

I never saw Grace cry until the day I told her we were going to leave Kenya. When the day to leave came, she stood at the market with us, holding my hand until the *matatu* came. The four of us climbed in with our bags and backpacks, squeezing in among other travelers to sit on the benches that lined both sides of the truck.

Through the dirty window I caught a glimpse of Grace, crying. And then the *matatu* sped away.

Beside me a woman held a cloth bag with a chicken inside. Only its head poked out. As the *matatu* rattled and bumped along, the woman kept a tight grip on the bag, and the chicken did not make a sound. I knew what lay ahead of me about as well as the bird knew what lay ahead of it. The chicken stared at me with one hard bright eye, while the only life I knew slipped farther and farther behind us.

. . . . .

I explained as much of this to the class as I could. I didn't really describe the day we left on the *matatu* or the chicken staring at me. But those things were in my mind while my voice was only explaining how *matatus* are like buses, except they're pickup trucks with a roof over the back. The man who takes your money waits till everyone has gotten on, and then he jumps onto the back bumper, holding onto the rack on top, slaps the side of the truck and yells, "Twende!"—"Let's go!"—and then the driver takes off.

I did tell them about Grace, because Mr. Inayatullah asked me if I had a best friend there and what kinds of things we did together. All the African American kids hooted when I talked about trying to do rows in Grace's hair and Grace trying to do mine. There are twenty-two kids in this class, and only four of them are African American. They stand out the way Faith and I stood out at Shibuye.

There's another kid who stands out, in a different way. His name is Brian, and he doesn't talk very much. At least he hasn't so far. He has short blond hair, so light it's almost white, and his eyes are pale blue, and I've never seen anyone so awkward and nervous.

When we're going somewhere, like walking to music or art or lunch, Brian is always stumbling and tripping over things. In class, he's always fidgeting with something on his desk, like a pencil or eraser or something he's pulled out of his pocket, maybe a bottle cap or a keychain. He doesn't look at the other students very much when he does this. It's almost like he's trying not to see the rest of us. Or maybe he doesn't want us to see him.

Sometimes he'll make an annoying noise while he's fidgeting. People will start looking around to see where it's coming from, and then Mr. Inayatullah tells him to put the thing away. He turns red, and somehow he drops the thing and has to pick it up off the floor before he can put it away.

Yesterday when the noise started—this time he was clicking a pencil sharpener against his desktop—Mr. Inayatullah paused beside Brian's desk. Mr. In had been pacing around the room, talking about book reports. He didn't stop talking about the reports, and he didn't look at Brian either, but he laid his hand over Brian's hand for a few seconds, silencing the clicking. Then he moved on. Brian put his hands in his lap.

While I was talking about my old school, most of the kids looked really interested. Even Brian was watching me instead of keeping his eyes on the blue rug. The kids stared hard at each picture before passing it on, and they asked a lot of questions.

"Didn't you hate wearing a uniform?"

"Did you see any lions?"

"Giraffes?"

"Tigers?"

"Was it really hot all the time?"

"Did you live in a jungle?"

"Did you ever get to see movies?"

Brian didn't ask anything. Neither did Sylvan.

I answered as many questions as I could, until Mr. Inayatullah said we had to go to music.

On the way to music, down the long tiled hall, I was almost skipping. I felt happier than I ever had in this school so far. Now they would understand me, I thought. Now they would like me.

But it didn't turn out to be quite that simple.

chapter five

SYLVAN

I woke up Saturday morning in my room in
Will's apartment, and for a second I just saw
a white ceiling and didn't know where I was.
Then I woke up a little more and looked around,
and it all made sense. There was my backpack
on the floor, along with the clothes I'd worn
on Friday. There was the desk I never used,
and there was the bookcase that never seemed
to have whatever book I was looking for because I'd left it at Lila's. There was the little

bedside table and the lamp with a base shaped like a sailboat.

Almost everything in Will's apartment was new, because when he moved out of our house, he didn't take any furniture. I think he wanted everything to be completely different, you know? Because he moved to this huge apartment building with a swimming pool in the back. The inside was all clean and white, and the stove and refrigerator and all those kitchen things were shiny and new. The whole place was about as different from home—Lila's old house, with the chickens out back—as any place could possibly be.

I lay in bed for a few minutes, just listening to all the soft apartment noises—a door shutting hard, water running, a voice in the hall. Everything sounded muffled, like the apartment was wrapped in an enormous fluffy blanket.

The clock beside the bed told me it was 7:10, which meant that Will would sleep for another hour and Justin for about four more. It was bright outside, and I hoped it would get warm enough to swim in the pool.

I rolled out of bed and went to the living room and turned on the TV. I found a cartoon channel and flopped down on the thick blue carpet to watch. Lila didn't have a TV, so I watched as much as I could at Will's. Last weekend Will and Justin got mad at me because I turned it on too loud and woke them up, so this time I was super careful to keep the sound low.

Being at Will's was like being on vacation—TV, a pool, and no chores, because a cleaning lady came every Tuesday. Will and I usually got pizza on Saturday night. Justin too, if he was around, but sometimes he was out with his friends.

Lila got all grumpy one day last spring when I told her how fun it was there, so I stopped saying much about it. I just told her about all the homework I did there. Most weekends Mr. Fitzpatrick didn't give much homework, really, but when I came back to Lila's house on Sunday nights, sometimes it seemed like homework was the only safe thing to talk about.

. . . . .

I'd only been watching cartoons for a few minutes when I heard Will rattling around in the kitchen. I wanted to ask him what he wanted to do that day, but it's better not to ask Will anything until he's had a cup of coffee. I switched the channel to an old *Scooby-Doo* and forgot about Will until he sat down on the floor behind me with his back against the couch. "How's the Scooby dog?" he asked.

"Good," I said. An ad came on, so I rolled over on my back to look at him. Suddenly he grabbed my ankles and pulled me toward him across the carpet. My shirt came up to my armpits, and Will pretended to punch my bare stomach. I was laughing so much that when I fakepunched back at him, I missed completely. He pulled me up in a hug, and I felt his rough cheek against my ear.

"Where you been all week, tiger?"

"At school. At home."

"Naah, I don't believe it. You sure you weren't in Vegas? Playing blackjack and pulling the one-arm bandits?"

"What are we doing today?"

He looked surprised. "Same thing we always do. Drink some whisky, play poker, maybe hold up a 7-Eleven."

"Will, come on. I want to *do* something."

"Like what?"

"I don't know. Let's wake up Justin and see if he wants to go for a bike ride or something."

Will shook his head. "Justin was up way too late last night. I don't think he'd appreciate being waked up this early. How about you and me do something?"

A half hour later we were in Will's car, heading for the state forest to take a hike. A few years ago, all four of us used to take hikes together. Or go biking or kayaking. We all liked that kind of thing, but Will was the one who got everybody moving.

Will is an outdoors kind of guy. His favorite things are biking, hiking, and camping, and his job is running a store that sells that kind of stuff—bicycles, tents, sleeping bags, kayaks, hiking boots, running shoes, nature books. He and his partner, Steve, own the store, and four or five other people work for them. I think it's cool that they own it, but Will says being an owner mainly means you work twice as hard as anyone else.

Sometimes he has to work part of the weekend, but only if one of his employees gets sick. Most of the time Steve and the other people run the store on the weekend. Will worked it out with them so that he could hang out with Justin and me almost every Saturday and Sunday.

We hiked about an hour and a half, up and down hills, through quiet woods alongside a creek. I liked how clean the air smelled, so far away from cars and trucks. Once a snake slipped across the trail in front of us, so fast I couldn't focus on it. All I saw were lightning-fast S's flowing between bushes. It was probably a garter snake, Will said.

We stopped at the base of a waterfall and looked up. It wasn't very high for a waterfall— maybe three or four times my height—but it was full and rushing and made a lot of noise as the water hurtled down the rocks. I picked up a stick and threw it as high up the falls as I could, then tried to follow it with my eyes. I lost sight of it in the tumble of water at the bottom, then saw it again a second later, floating in the creek below the falls.

We sat on some big rocks just off the trail, and Will took off his backpack and pulled out granola bars and water bottles. For a few minutes we sat there without a word, just eating our snack and watching the waterfall. I felt so good there, with Will and the waterfall and the trees and no need to talk—just the sound of the water.

. . . . .

At school on Monday, Charity started talking to me on the way to the lunchroom. "Kyle said you were at the protest about the deer on Friday."

"Yeah," I muttered, hoping nobody else had heard her.

"Did you carry a sign?"

"Only because Lila made me."

"Don't you like doing things like that?"

"No," I said, loud enough that Lucy turned around in front of me with a curious look.

As soon as we got our food, I went over to a table full of boys and squeezed in between Adam and Peter.

"Hey, Tree Boy," Adam said with his mouth full of peanut butter and jelly. "I think Charity likes you."

"No, she doesn't. You're crazy." I opened my milk carton and tried to not look at Adam.

"Then why does she talk to you all the time?" he said. "It's so obvious."

Peter was talking to Eli across the table, so they weren't listening to Adam. I hoped no one else was.

"She doesn't like me. And I don't like her."

"Oh yeah, sure. Want me to tell everybody about it?" Adam said with a wicked grin.

"Just shut up, Adam! You better not say stuff like that if you want to be my friend."

"OK, fine," he said reluctantly.

"Promise you won't go around saying that."

"OK, Tree Boy, OK," he said and started shoveling in spoonfuls of applesauce.

I wondered if he'd really keep his promise.

Adam was my friend, but sometimes he kind of liked to cause trouble.

. . . . .

The next day Charity told us about her school in Kenya. I already knew some of it because of what she and her mom said the night they came over for dinner. But at school she had pictures too, and she passed them around.

There was Charity in the middle of a group of African girls, all dressed in blue skirts and shirts, standing in front of a building with a roof like the wavy inside part of a thick piece of cardboard.

There was the market, where Charity said they went to buy vegetables and eggs and things like soap or thread or matches. The market wasn't a building, just a place where people spread bright cloths on the ground and set out on top all the things they had to sell.

There was Charity's mom at the clinic where she was a nurse. She didn't look as thin and tired as she did the night she came to our house. In the picture she was talking to a woman holding a baby that looked sick.

The pictures made me want to go to another continent too. It would be so cool to live for a while in a place where everything was completely different from what you were used to. The people, the weather, the language, everything you saw around you—totally new. I wondered if I would feel like a new person in a place like that. I wasn't sure, but I liked the idea. Just get on a plane, cross the ocean, and not be Sylvan anymore.

. . . . .

That afternoon Adam came over after school, and we played soccer in the backyard. It was another sunny day, and after being stuck in school all day, it felt great to run and kick and yell insults at each other. We went up and down the half of the yard that wasn't fenced in for the chickens, shoving with our shoulders and tangling our legs as we fought for control of the ball. Sometimes the ball got loose and slammed into the fence, and the chickens would squawk and scramble away. They were so funny, like fat old ladies in a tizzy about something. The first time it happened, Adam and I dropped to the ground laughing.

Zachary was lying nearby watching us, but after the ball banged into the fence, he got up and strolled off in a snooty way.

I was racing after the ball when somebody a lot bigger hurtled past me, stretched out a long leg, and stole it.

"Hey!" I yelled.

Justin dribbled the ball up and down the field, practically dancing around Adam and me as we tried to get it back. Justin's hair is dark brown like mine but long and shaggy, and he kept sweeping it back out of his eyes.

Suddenly he stopped, one foot on top of the ball, and said, "Oh, did you guys want this ball?" He gave the ball a nudge toward us and headed for the house, scooping up his backpack on the way.

"Your brother is cool," Adam said after the door closed behind Justin.

I thought so too, but I only shrugged and gave the ball a kick to get things going again.

After a while we were getting hot and sweaty, so we came inside for lemonade. We poured ourselves tall glasses and sank into the saggy old couch.

"Wish you had video games, Tree Boy," Adam said.

"Me too." I picked up a Slinky from the coffee table and let it ripple back and forth between my hands. "We could play a computer game."

"Naah."

After a minute I said, "Do you like Mr. In?"

"Yeah, he's cool," Adam replied. "Only I can't believe he gave us homework the very first week."

"We got a pretty good class this year," I said. "We got Peter and Eli, and we didn't get Bridget and Amanda—the most annoying girls on the planet."

"Yeah, but we got Charity," Adam said. "She's weirder than both of them put together."

"I know, but it was kind of cool, seeing pictures from Africa."

"Kind of," Adam said with a shrug. Then he grinned. "I can't believe she shakes the teacher's hand all the time."

"Yeah, and she thinks we should have a prayer in school every day."

"You know what's really wrong with that girl?"

"What?"

"She's a P.K.," Adam said. "Preacher's kid. I knew a couple of them in my old school. They think they're supposed to be perfect, like saints or something, and they're always total nerds. Except some of them are the exact opposite—they get in trouble all the time."

That kind of made sense.

I drained my lemonade.

But then I remembered that Charity's father said he was done with all that—he wasn't a pastor anymore. I told Adam about that.

He shrugged again. "There goes her excuse. I guess she's just weird." He set down his glass. "Come on, let's go back outside."

· · · · ·

"Today," Mr. In told us, smiling and rocking back and forth from his heels to his toes, "we're going to start a big project for social studies."

By this time we'd been in fifth grade for

more than a month. In fourth grade, when I'd hear words like "big project," my stomach would sink through the floor. But I never felt that way with Mr. In. He got so excited that he made you feel like you were *lucky* to get to do this project.

His tie was red as usual that day, but it had tiny flags, all different, scattered across it. That turned out to be a clue to the project.

"This unit is called 'Explore the World,'" Mr. In continued. "It's a chance to get to know some of the major countries around the world. We're going to hear what their languages and their music sound like, see what their landscapes and cities look like, find out what people do there to make a living, what they wear, what they eat—all kinds of things.

"I'm going to show you a slide show I've made, just to give you a taste of what these countries are like. And then I'll ask you to write down which ones you're interested in learning more about. And then I'll pair you up so you can work in teams of two to prepare a presentation, so the whole class can learn from you."

I looked at Charity. I was sure she was thinking that she could pick Kenya, and this project would be a piece of cake. But Mr. In killed that idea.

"Your choices won't include every country in the world," he said. "I'd like to have a sampling of large countries from each continent, so I've made a list of sixteen. There are twenty-two students in the class, so we'll have eleven teams. With sixteen countries to choose from, I'm hoping that everyone will get an assignment that will interest them."

He gazed around the room, taking time to look us all over. "Of course, I want this to be a *learning* experience. For everybody. So my list does not include the United States. Or Kenya," he added with a smiling glance at Charity. "Or Korea," he said, looking at Mia, whose parents came from there and took her back to visit every summer.

The slide show was cool. I mean, I was interested in almost all the countries. I didn't want to make presentations about them—I just wanted to go and see them. China, Japan, India, France,

South Africa, Egypt, Brazil, Australia, Russia . . . they all sounded so different from regular old America. I imagined myself at eighteen. I'd be out of school and totally free, traveling all over the world with nothing but a backpack.

At the end Mr. In told us to write down our first three choices and number them. "Without talking, please. I want to know what interests *you*, not what you hope will get you teamed up with your best friend."

Lucy and Melissa mouthed words at each other when Mr. In wasn't looking. So did a few other best friends. I hoped I'd get someone I liked for a partner, but mostly I was thinking about which countries to pick. Finally, I wrote down, "1. Australia, 2. Nigeria, 3. Brazil."

Mr. In collected the pieces of paper, and then we went to PE. On the way everybody chattered about what countries they'd picked.

Adam rattled off Japan, India, and Egypt.

"Aww," I said. "Mine are all different."

"Yeah. I hope I get a good partner. And I really hope I get Japan. My cousin went there once, and he brought back all these cool pictures and things."

By then we had reached the gym, and Adam grabbed a basketball so he could take a few shots before the PE teacher told him to put it away. I stood watching him as he pounded toward the basket.

Charity came up beside me. "Guess what countries I wrote down."

"Um, I don't know," I muttered.

Suddenly the PE teacher called out to everyone to come to the sideline. Relieved, I said, "Hey, we gotta line up," and hurried over to the group.

· · · · ·

When we got back to the classroom after PE, Mr. In told us he'd figured out our teams for the international project. He started reading his list. Melissa and Rob got Nigeria. Lucy and Deena got France. India went to Adam and Charity.

Adam looked at me and rolled his eyes, and I grinned back at him. Then I saw Charity looking our way. She must have seen Adam's eye-rolling, because she turned her face to the front, really quick. I felt kind of bad for her.

But seconds later I forgot about that, because Mr. In read out my assignment. I got Australia, my first choice—great. But who did I get for a partner? Brian Laidlaw, a.k.a. the Trampoline Kid.

I was pretty worried about what it would be like to do a major project with Brian. I didn't know him very well—no one did. He didn't say much, and he was no good at games like dodgeball or kickball, so even at recess he stayed off by himself. He acted nervous all the time.

I even wondered if he was retarded or something. Like, was he smart enough to do regular schoolwork? Could he handle his part of a big project like this? I realized I had no idea what it was like to be inside Brian Laidlaw's head.

• • • • •

Adam and I played soccer at his house that day after school. It was cold, and snowflakes kept fluttering down without ever getting serious. We chased each other up and down his backyard, with the fence at each end for a goal. The grass was damp and sprinkled with leaves, even though Adam and his mom had raked up big piles over the weekend.

When we'd had enough, we headed in. While we were taking our shoes off, just inside the back door, Adam said, "This project Mr. In is giving us is gonna *suck*. It'll take forever, and I have to do it with Preacher Girl."

"Well," I said as we went into the kitchen, "'I bet it's a lot easier to work with Preacher Girl than the Trampoline Kid."

"Oh yeah, I forgot," Adam said, pouring glasses of milk for us. "You got a weird partner too."

"Is he even *normal*?" I wondered. "Or is he retarded or something?"

"Developmentally disabled," Adam corrected me. "That's what you're supposed to say. My dad works with kids like that."

"OK, developmentally disabled. But is he? Because if he is, I don't know how we're going to do this project together."

"He's not," Adam said confidently. "He got a hundred on the last math test—I saw his paper when Mr. In was handing them back."

That was a relief. But I still couldn't imagine me and Brian talking about this project and planning it together.

We went into Adam's living room to play video games.

"Why did you pick India, anyway?" I asked as we unwrapped the wires around the controllers.

"I just wanted to know about snake charmers. Like, can they really do that—play a flute and the snake comes up out of the basket? Or is that just something you see in cartoons?"

"I don't know."

"Well, that's all I wanted to know about India," Adam said glumly. "But I guess I'm going to find out a whole lot more."

· · · · ·

For the next three weeks we used all our social studies time to work on the projects. In the library we used books and the Internet to find information. We took notes on what we read, and we had to turn these in for Mr. In to look over, because we were supposed to be learning how to take good notes.

Each team had a folder on one of the computers in the library, where we saved articles about the country, maps, pictures of its flag, and photos of people and places. Mr. In made us gather facts about the kind of government in the country, the kind of money used there, the climate, geography, the crops they grow, natural resources like minerals and trees, and the industries like steel or textile manufacturing. Plus we had to find a folktale from our country.

Does that sound like a lot of work? It was. It was a *huge* amount of work. And for some of us, having a partner didn't make it any easier.

chapter six

CHARITY

I wrote a letter to Grace on a cold day in early
December. I'd been writing to her at least once
a week since we moved to America. In the first
few letters I told her how strange everything
was—my grandparents' house, then our house.
Later, I wrote about how school was so different
and how the kids didn't like me. How everyone
has a lot more things here, but they aren't very
friendly, and they live in small families without
any grandparents or cousins, sometimes just

three or four people in a huge house.

This time I told her about the snow and drew pictures of snowflakes at the top of my letter. There was only a little snow—it wasn't even sticking to the ground much—but it was fun to describe it to Grace. I pictured her smiling as she tried to imagine the sight and feel of cold white flakes dropping from the sky.

I told her I still didn't like school, but I was getting used to doing things the way American kids did. I didn't stand up to speak to the teacher anymore or shake his hand when I went into the classroom in the morning. I'd memorized the Pledge of Allegiance, and I liked the rhythm of it, though saying it wasn't nearly as nice as singing "Eh Mungu Nguvu Yetu" each morning.

I just needed a couple of kids to be real friends with, and so far I hadn't found anybody. Mom said that finding friends just takes a little while when you're new. But it already seemed like we'd been here a long time.

Grace wrote to me too, but not as often, and her letters were always short. I could understand why. She had a lot of chores to do at home, so she didn't have much time. Also, she didn't speak English at home, so writing in English was hard for her. Sometimes she would use a completely wrong word, and I'd have to figure out what she meant. And besides all that, airmail stamps cost money. Grace was probably trying not to use too many of the ones Mom and I had given her before we left. Grace's family didn't have extra money for anything they didn't absolutely need, like food and clothes.

I loved getting letters from her, but they always made me feel homesick for Shibuye. Even if we were all uneasy there, toward the end.

· · · · ·

It's hard to explain how much the church spire meant to my father. The church had been built by some other missionaries years before us, and it was the largest building for miles, bigger even than the school. It was made of ordinary concrete blocks, but it was tall and massive, and it even had colored glass in the big window behind the altar.

Inside, there weren't any pews for people to sit in. There were a few benches along the sides, but most people stood up. The ceiling was really high, and on Sunday mornings the church echoed with singing and clapping and drumming.

People came to church on foot, of course—no one had a car. They walked along red-brown dirt roads and narrow paths that wound through fields of maize and sugarcane. Around the church was a grassy lawn. When the grass got too high, the caretaker, Mr. Kafuna, cut it with a scythe. There were lots of trees around the church too. The ones I liked best were the Nandi flame trees, with big orange flowers.

A small grove of trees separated the church from two houses—one where we lived and one that Mom had turned into a clinic. Often I woke up early in the morning to the sound of voices chatting in Luhya outside, where people waited for their turn to see Mom.

Even though the church seemed tall when you stood beside it, it couldn't be seen from far away, because it sat on low ground and had trees on three sides of it. So Dad decided the church needed a spire. He talked about a tall, slender tower on the peak of the roof, with a cross at the very top of it, so that people for miles around would know the church was there. On their way to the market or wherever, the spire would remind them of the church and its Sunday services. They would see how it pointed upward, and would think of heaven and the kingdom of God.

Dad occasionally mentioned the idea of getting a spire during our first four years in Kenya. And it made sense to me—after all, the American churches I remembered all had something like that on top. But he was always busy with one project or another. It wasn't until our last year in Africa that he got serious about it.

We didn't know that was going to be our last year in Africa. And we certainly didn't know that, in a way, it was the spire that would send us back across the ocean.

. . . . .

The reason Dad got serious about the spire was that things weren't going very well with the church. For one thing, every Sunday the big building was half empty.

When we first came to Kenya, plenty of people were coming to church. The pastor before Dad was really popular—people always talked about how kind Reverend Fisher was and how funny and clever he was and how he spoke Luhya better than any white person they'd ever seen. He was killed in a car accident, and people told us about it with tears in their eyes.

Everyone welcomed us politely, though. They seemed curious about us. But after a while, a lot of them stopped coming to church. Dad got worried. He started working harder and harder, at the church and at the co-op, where he and the farmers worked together to sell their crops and figure out the best ways to grow more.

He traveled for miles, talking to everybody and asking them to join the co-op and come to church. He spent more time helping Mom in the clinic. He visited sick people and prayed with them. He tried to make the services better, with more African music, more singing and dancing. He even bought drums.

Then he started something new—a big feast for everyone after the Christmas and Easter services. Each time, Mom and Dad bought a sheep and a couple of goats and big bags of cornmeal and beans, and they paid a few women to cook everything. The Africans loved it, and so did Faith and I. Everybody was in a good mood, there was music from radios, and all the kids ran around playing together.

It seemed like everything Dad was doing was beginning to help—more people were going to church and the co-op. But then, at the feast last Easter, there was one very big problem.

A lot of the men in the village really like to drink beer, either the homemade kind or the Tusker that comes in big brown bottles. But of course Dad didn't allow drinking at the church feasts. That would be completely inappropriate.

But last Easter four of the men showed up drunk. They hadn't been in church like the rest of us—they'd been home drinking. And they weren't just a little tipsy. They were what Mom called "roaring drunk." They were singing and stumbling around with their arms across one another's shoulders, bumping into people, and making a lot of noise.

Most people just laughed or ignored them, but Dad got absolutely furious. His big voice boomed out "Hey!" and he strode through the crowd toward the drunk men. Everyone else got out of his way and watched. I was helping Mom set out plates and cups on a table, but at the sound of Dad's shout, we both froze.

Dad planted himself in front of the men and started yelling at them in a mixture of English, Luhya, and Swahili, a language every Kenyan knows, at least a little bit.

"This is disgraceful. You're all drunk, *kabisa*"—totally. "How dare you show up like this at church on this holy day—get out! You are not welcome here."

The four drunk men watched him, swaying a little with their arms around one another.

They were listening but half laughing, like boys at school being scolded by a teacher they're not afraid of. Then one of them stepped forward. He was a skinny man with a slightly squashed-looking nose, and his forehead had angry lines that pressed down on his eyebrows. He spat on the ground in front of Dad.

"*Mzungu!*" he yelled. "You think we are your slaves. You think you give orders to African men. You think we must obey you." And he spat again.

I moved a step closer to Mom, my heart beating fast.

"You want we call you *bwana*. I call you—!" The last word was an African word I didn't know. It must have meant something really bad.

The crowd murmured, and a woman called out in a sharp voice, "Keep quiet, Albert—you do not know what you are saying."

Farther back in the crowd, a man said loudly, "We must welcome our visitors—we must not abuse them." Other voices echoed, "*Ndiyo*, yes."

It seemed like the people were on Dad's side, because Albert was being so rude. I hoped Albert would realize that and just go away.

But he wasn't finished. "Leave our country!" he bellowed. "Here we do not want you—go back to America!"

I shivered, but Dad answered in his thunder voice. "Who are you to tell a servant of the Lord to leave this place?"

They stood face-to-face, glaring at each other. They were about the same height, but Dad looked a lot stronger.

"Who am I? I am African man!" Albert took a step toward Dad, waving his fist, but one of his drunk friends and another man grabbed his arms and pulled him back, saying "*Ngoja, ngoja*"—wait, wait.

"You're not a man. You're a drunken fool," Dad said. A few people laughed, but others frowned.

And then one of the other drunks spoke up, pointing an angry finger at Dad. This man was tall, with a long scar on his cheek. He was swaying a little but kept his eyes on Dad as he spat out the words. "You—no call this man a fool."

"When I see a jackal, I do not call it a lion."

More people laughed this time, but on some other faces the frowns grew deeper. And the drunk men looked even angrier than before.

I guess maybe Dad should have stopped right there. Maybe everyone would have calmed down. But Dad has always hated drinking, and I guess he hated the way these people were interrupting his feast. So he kept on going.

"Go back to your homes," he ordered. "You cannot come to the feast in this condition. You cannot come here drunk. Go home!"

"You do not tell us what we must do!" Albert shouted.

But one of the drunk men who hadn't said anything so far now spoke up. "*Twende*"—let's go—he said to his friends. "What do we want with this white man's feast?"

"Yes," the scarred man answered loudly. "It is a white man's feast. I will not eat his food." And he clamped his hand on Albert's shoulder, and all four of the men turned and left, muttering.

Dad turned to the crowd, looking

triumphant, and said, "Let us rejoice in the risen Christ, and enjoy our time together as Christian friends."

He waved toward the tables of food, and people began to take plates as Mom and some other women filled them. But the happy feast-day mood had been spoiled, and there were a lot of angry looks in Dad's direction.

The next Sunday, the congregation was smaller than ever. And some people weren't so friendly to us after that Easter day. Still, Dad felt that he had done the right thing, sending the drunk men away. And soon after that, he decided the church would have a spire, one way or another.

"It's a symbol," he said. "It will show that the church is strong."

. . . . .

Getting a spire wasn't easy, because there was no money for one. First, Dad decided to ask our group of churches in America. The churches already gave money to Dad and Mom every month, so that we could buy food and clothes and gas for the car. They also gave money to pay Mr. Kafuna, buy medicine and bandages for the clinic, and cover all kinds of other things, like repairing the church roof.

Mom and Dad said the money was always stretched thin, because there were so many serious needs in Shibuye. People needed rain barrels and wells, so the women wouldn't always have to carry buckets of water on their heads from the streams. The clinic needed more equipment and supplies. And when the crops were small, people needed more to eat. They'd save what they could by eating only one or two meals a day. Mom and Dad would try to get sacks of maize meal or beans from some aid agency or buy it themselves, so they could share it with people around Shibuye.

The government ran the primary school that Faith and I attended, but it had very few books and hardly anything to use for science experiments. There were chalkboards, but teachers brought only a piece or two of chalk to the classrooms. They kept the rest in the staff room so it wouldn't disappear. And of course there weren't any computers.

The people who came to Mom for medical care didn't have to pay, but most of them were so grateful that they tried to pay somehow, bringing her a couple of eggs or a mango or a few *ndizi*, tiny sweet bananas. Mom did whatever she could for them, and sometimes she or Dad used our car to take them to the hospital, far off in Kisumu.

We had a car, we had books in our house, we never had to skip meals. Those were some of the ways we were better off than most of the Africans. But *Americans*, Dad would say in disgust—look at how much they had and how little they were willing to share with Shibuye.

He said it as if we weren't Americans, as if we were completely different from those people far off in the United States. And I really didn't feel like an American. Of course I was different from the African girls I played with, but still, I felt like a Kenyan—a special kind of Kenyan, maybe, but still a Kenyan.

One afternoon Mom drove to the village a few miles away to do some errands. The church had a post office box there, and she brought back a few letters. There was one from Grandma addressed to me and Faith. Since Faith was playing outside, I got to read it first. I sat on the bench beside the table and ripped it open. We didn't get much mail, so any letter from America was at least a little bit exciting.

Mom handed the other envelopes to Dad, and he sorted through them before choosing one to open. Absorbed in Grandma's letter, I wasn't paying any attention to Dad—until his fist crashed down on the table, and I almost jumped out of my skin.

"*What?*" Mom and I said at the same instant.

"They won't fund it," he growled. "They won't pay for the spire."

His face was red, and he was breathing heavily. "Hypocrites. Drive their SUVs right up to their big churches with the million-dollar fitness centers. And they can't buy one thin little spire for a poor church in Africa?"

He threw the letter down on the table and stood there clenching his fists. "This is *my* church. I don't *have* a gym to draw people in. I don't *have* a big budget to toss around." He was silent a moment, breathing hard.

"I decide what this church needs, and I've decided it needs a spire. And it's going to get one."

He stomped out of the house, fast, his long mane of hair flying.

· · · · ·

After that Dad was in a bad mood for weeks. The first time I saw him looking more cheerful was the day Faith and I came home from school and found him and Mr. Kafuna behind the church looking at a big pile of lumber.

"What's this?" I asked.

"It's the spire for the church. Or at least it will be," Dad answered, smiling.

"Did someone give us money for it?"

"Not exactly." Dad explained that he had paid for half of it and the seller had given him a few months to pay the rest. He didn't have enough money left to hire a carpenter to build the spire, but he and Mr. Kafuna were going to build it themselves.

I looked at Mr. Kafuna. His wrinkled face showed nothing but the respectful look he always wore while listening to Dad. Mr. Kafuna had always fixed and cleaned things around the church, but I couldn't remember either him or Dad ever building anything.

Still, I felt hopeful as Faith and I went to the house. It was nice to see Dad looking happier. He and Mr. Kafuna together, I told myself, could probably make anything they set their minds to.

· · · · ·

Weeks went by before the spire began to take shape. Dad had to go around to some other churches to borrow tools. Sometimes he could only keep them for a few days because the lenders needed them, and he'd have to wait until the tools were available again. He and Mr. Kafuna worked on the spire whenever they had time, sawing, hammering, pausing often to peer at their sketches and pencil in corrections or new ideas.

Because the finished spire would be too heavy to hoist up to the roof, they were building it in pieces. They planned to take the pieces up to the roof one by one, putting them together up there.

Soon after they began working on the pieces, downpours started happening almost every afternoon. On school days we loved the rain, because the tremendous noise of the drops hurtling onto the metal roof of the school meant that teachers couldn't teach. They might frown, or they might smile, but there was nothing they could do until the rain stopped. We kids would chatter as loud as we could or, if we felt like it, lay our heads down on the desk, where we could almost feel the pounding of the rain, and wait.

Building the spire became the only thing Dad ever talked about. He stopped making prayer visits to sick people and spent less and less time at the co-op or helping Mom in the clinic, even though she needed his help.

Sick and injured people came to her from far beyond our little community because they had heard that she had medicine and would help them for free. There were always people waiting outside the clinic, and sometimes she went to visit people who were too sick to come to her. Dad wasn't a nurse or a doctor, but he could fetch things that Mom needed, put on bandages, take a person's temperature, or drive someone to the hospital.

"Martin," she said one day, "you're forgetting what's important. You're forgetting what we're here for."

. . . . .

The first time Dad and Mr. Kafuna climbed up to work on the roof was a sunny Saturday morning. The sky was pale blue, and a light breeze was blowing off and on.

They had built a short, crude ladder, then nailed and lashed it to a bigger ladder, adding four or five more steps to it. Faith and I stood there watching as they positioned the extra-long ladder against the side of the church.

Dad went first. With a cloth bag of tools over one shoulder, he climbed slowly, the ladder creaking. When his weight came down on the first rung of the homemade part, it creaked so loud I gasped, afraid it was about to break. But Dad kept on going, and in a moment he had crawled onto the roof.

He crouched there, leaning away from the edge, while Mr. Kafuna began to climb up, holding a piece of the spire's base. Mr. Kafuna climbed much more slowly than Dad. After a few steps he paused and looked around. He seemed nervous.

"Charity," he said quietly. "Please hold this ladder. It is shaking."

So I went over and held the ladder as steady as I could. Mr. Kafuna smiled at me and began climbing again, the big piece of wood clamped under one arm. When he got high enough to put his free hand on the roof's edge, he lifted the piece onto the roof, and Dad dragged it up to the crest.

"You girls stand back," he called down to us. "In case I drop anything."

Faith came over to me and held my hand.

I stared up at Dad on the peak of the roof. He was hammering the piece of wood into the shingles with long hard swings of his arm. A loud bang sounded each time the hammer struck the nail. Against the bright sky his face was dark, but his hair glowed gold in the sun, and the wind blew it back in a stream.

Bwana Simba, I thought. He looked like a king up there.

. . . . .

It was a few more days before they were ready to put the final piece in place, the long pole with a cross on the end of it. They didn't work on Sunday, the day of rest, and sometimes they had to wait out the rain, or the paint had to dry. Dad told us the wood had to be painted, to protect it from rain and wind, so it wouldn't rot. Together he and Mr. Kafuna had chosen the color—bright yellow.

"Very beautiful," Mr. Kafuna had said a few days earlier, smiling, after Dad had painted the first piece. They both stood over it as it lay in the grass, gleaming and wet.

"If I could gild it with real gold, like a

cathedral in Europe, I would," Dad said. "But a bright sunny yellow is close enough."

He and Mr. Kafuna both looked proud. They glanced up at the roof as if they imagined the spire shining there.

Now that the spire was taking shape, I could see that it wasn't as elegant as the ones on churches in America. The base wasn't smoothly curved and did not merge gracefully into the highest and narrowest parts. But it still had a brave, triumphant look about it, I thought, or at least it would when the final piece went up. It would be so tall and bright, so high above the trees, on top of the tallest building for miles around.

Dad went around looking almost satisfied, eager for the final step. He decided to make a ceremony of it. He and Mr. Kafuna would raise the cross early on Sunday morning, before services, and everyone could come and watch, then go to church in a mood to celebrate.

On Sunday morning people gathered outside the church. Dad welcomed everybody and said a short prayer. Then he climbed up the ladder, and Mr. Kafuna handed up the long yellow pole with the yellow cross on top. People laughed and pointed and chatted, and the cross waved high in the air as Dad, standing with one foot on each side of the crest, tried to fit it into its holder.

The cross made the spire top-heavy, and it was hard for him to maneuver. After a minute or so, he seemed to get it in the right place, but it leaned and wobbled when he tried to put in the screws to hold it tight. Finally, he called to Mr. Kafuna to come up and help.

Mr. Kafuna hesitated, then shook his head with an anxious smile. I had never once seen him on the roof—he only climbed partway up the ladder and handed things to Dad. I knew he was afraid to go up so high.

"It is too high for me," he said. "Some other person can go there to help."

Dad's voice wasn't exactly commanding, but it was very firm. "We built this spire together, you and me. You should be proud to finish it. You will have the honor of putting in the last screw. Climb up here with me."

Other people called, "Yes, Kafuna! Go on, you can do it."

So at last Mr. Kafuna started up the ladder, with everyone watching. As he neared the roof his steps grew slower and slower. He stopped, hands clenched on the ladder, eyes level with the roof edge.

"You can do it," Dad said.

The crowd yelled and cheered.

I guess Mr. Kafuna couldn't turn back then, with all those eyes on him. He moved a hand up to the roof. He took one more step up the ladder and stopped again.

I was standing beside Grace. As Mr. Kafuna hesitated, she squeezed my hand. "He is afraid so much," she whispered to me. We were close enough to see the fear in his face. I felt bad for him. Probably he had never thought he'd have to do something like this, ever in his whole life.

But he went on, and he made it onto the roof. He crawled up the expanse toward Dad and the spire, with Dad grinning and calling encouragement.

My eyes hurt from staring up into the brightness of the almost cloudless sky.

Mr. Kafuna had reached the base of the spire and was holding on tight. Dad stood over him, holding the spire straight up.

Kneeling, Mr. Kafuna picked up a screwdriver and began trying to fasten the pole into the base. Everything was taking a while, I thought, but everyone in the crowd seemed patient and cheerful. The grown-ups chatted in Luhya while the little kids ran circles around them.

I glanced up at the roof again just in time to see the screwdriver drop from Mr. Kafuna's trembling hand and start to roll down the slope. He lunged to grab it and lost his balance. As the crowd cried out, he flailed toward the edge, his hands trying to seize anything. One hand caught the gutter, but his body was already tumbling over the edge. For a second he hung there by one hand. And then a six-foot section of gutter ripped away from the building, and Mr. Kafuna fell to the ground.

There was screaming and wailing as people rushed toward him, but I don't think Mr. Kafuna made a sound. I saw people make way for Mom to get to him, and then I lost sight of her pink shirt as the crowd closed in behind her.

Grace and I stood frozen. After a few seconds I realized my hands were hurting. My left hand was in Grace's, and we were squeezing each other's too tight. My right hand had folded into a fist, and my teeth were biting into it.

I looked for Dad and saw only his back as he hurried down the ladder. He had almost reached the bottom when a male voice, loud and anguished, rose over the crowd sounds with words that, for a moment, stopped everything: "He is dead!"

There was a second of silence and stillness, and then the men exclaiming, the women weeping and wailing, and Dad pushing his way through the crowd to get to Mr. Kafuna.

Faith pushed her head under my arm. She and Grace and I clung together, all of us crying. Through wet, blurry eyes I saw the yellow spire with the cross on top, so far away up there on top of the church, but leaning over to one side.

· · · · ·

Later, we had the Sunday morning service, sort of. Dad looked stunned, moving in slow motion, like he was underwater or sleepwalking. He said prayers. He said a few words about grief and the love of God. The people who usually led the singing started a mournful song. Many people were crying. Then Dad said the same words of farewell that he always said at the end, and the crowd slowly left.

Mom and Faith and I stood together in the back of the church while everyone walked out. Dad just kept standing in the front, under the cross, as if his thoughts were miles away. Mom led us toward him, but he headed out the side door.

We didn't see Dad all afternoon. He came home when it was almost completely dark, and he said almost nothing that night, though we tried to talk to him. The whole following week he hardly spoke. When Faith and I left for school on Monday morning, I couldn't keep my eyes away from the spot where Mr. Kafuna had died. I couldn't keep from glancing up at the spire, which didn't have a trace of the brave look it was meant to have.

The next Sunday Dad went to church earlier than the rest of us, as usual, to get everything ready. But when Mom and Faith and I walked in, the church was empty. Only the four of us stood in that big space, Dad at the far end, the rest of us just inside the door in the back.

"Where is everybody?" Faith asked Mom. Her little-kid voice echoed.

"I think maybe they're all too sad about Mr. Kafuna," Mom answered quietly, without even looking at Faith. She kept her eyes on Dad.

Slowly he walked toward us and stopped in front of Mom. "This is the end," he said in the same hollow, stunned voice that came out of him after Mr. Kafuna died.

"No," Mom said quickly. "No, Martin, it's not the end at all."

"There's nothing left."

"There is," she insisted. "God is still here. God's *work* is still here. A terrible thing happened, but it wasn't your fault. It can't separate you from the love of God."

He looked at her as if she was speaking a foreign language. He opened his mouth, then glanced down at me and Faith and closed it again. He walked past us and out the door. Once again we didn't see him for the whole afternoon.

That night was the night he didn't say grace at dinner, for the first time in my life. That was when he said we'd never say grace again.

None of us ate much, except Dad. Everyone but him seemed lost and confused. When Dad was finished, he put down his fork and said, "We're going back to America."

Seconds of silence went by. I heard the hoarse sound of the kerosene lantern, the chatter of insects outside.

"Martin," Mom said in a shaky voice, "that's something we'll discuss. And pray about. You can't just make an instant decision for all of us."

"My church is gone, Debbie. I was losing it anyway, and now it's gone. A good man is dead. I don't have anything to offer these people."

"You *do*, Martin. You have faith to offer them. Faith that guides us when things go wrong."

For a second he glanced at Faith, as if he'd suddenly noticed that she was named for something. Then he said, "You just don't get it, do you? I don't *have* faith anymore."

I felt like the ground under my feet had crumbled away.

chapter seven

SYLVAN

Brian Laidlaw is not a normal kid.

The first time we went to the library to work on our projects, I asked Brian if he wanted to look for Australia on the computer or find books about it.

"Computer," he said instantly. His voice was loud, and I saw the librarian glance toward us, but she didn't say anything.

"Well ..." I wanted the computer job too—searching the Internet sounded like more fun than looking for books. I waited for Brian to say "Is that OK with you?" or "But if you want to do the computer . . ." But he didn't say anything at all. He wasn't even looking at me. His eyes were darting all around the room, and he held his notebook close to his chest, like he was afraid someone would try to take it from him.

"OK," I sighed. "I'll find some books or an encyclopedia article or something. Then I'll come and find you."

He gave a jerky little nod and walked off toward the computers.

After a few minutes I found a couple of books about Australia, but they weren't very exciting—they were old, and the pictures were dull. One of them didn't even have pictures in color. The librarian, Ms. Kirsch, came over while I was looking at a page with photos of kangaroos and dingoes. She's young and has short, spiky blonde hair.

"Let me guess," Ms. Kirsch said. "Your project is about . . . Italy."

"Close," I said. "Are there any other books about Australia?"

"Don't give up on these," she said, tapping a bright red fingernail on one of them. "They're old, but they still have some good information. But I think we can find something more interesting."

She showed me a big book called *Cities around the World*, with a section on Sydney, and another book about the native people of Australia, who are called Aborigines. I'd never seen that word before. When I said it, I made it rhyme with *lines*, but Ms. Kirsch said to pronounce it with a *ridge* in the middle and *knees* at the end.

I got so interested in the Aborigines that I forgot all about Brian. Then Mr. In announced that we had five minutes left in the library, so I picked up the books and went to find him.

The library had a long row of computers along one wall, and kids from our class were using all of them. Brian was sitting at the last computer in the row.

When I came up to him, he jumped, like I'd sneaked up behind him or something.

"I found some pretty good books," I said.

"What did you find?"

"Oh. Not much."

I looked at his screen. On it was some kind of math game I'd never seen before.

"Didn't you search for Australia?"

"Uh, yeah." He seemed to be looking at the table, the screen, the wall—anywhere except at me.

"Well, did you find any good sites?"

"It was all boring."

"Did you save anything? Or print anything out?"

He shook his head. Then he kept shaking it for at least five seconds longer.

What a great partner, I thought.

"So you've just been sitting here playing games?"

"It's math. I'm doing math." He stared at the screen, and his hand twitched on the mouse.

"But—"

"Time to go," Mr. In called from the other side of the room. "If you need to check something out, do it now."

"Let me see the history," I demanded.

Brian got up and walked away. I quickly sat

down and opened the browser's history list. There was a search for Australia. But he hadn't visited a single Australia page after that. There was nothing else except the math game.

"Idiot," I muttered.

Then I took a closer look at the game. It looked like every time you solved a math problem and got it right, a tank or a bomb or something would explode. The problems looked really hard, but the screen was littered with piles of rubble where Brian had blown something up.

"Sylvan, Melissa, Adam—let's go," Mr. In said. Everyone else was at the door, ready to leave.

I grabbed my books and hurried over to Ms. Kirsch to check them out. The rule was that you had to close everything on your screen when you left, but I didn't bother. I was scowling as I waited for the person ahead of me to finish checking out. So Brian could solve hard math problems— good for him. But was he going to work on the social studies project, or was I going to have to do it all by myself?

· · · · ·

That afternoon during our science lesson, the classroom door creaked open. Our principal, Ms. Langley, poked her head in. She paused for a second, peering around the room.

I heard a couple of smothered giggles and rubbed my nose to hide my grin. She looked so funny—just her head stretched past the door, her wavy, gray-and-brown hair looking like she'd been out in a high wind, and a puzzled expression on her face. She was probably looking for Mr. In, but he had gone to the back of the room to set up the microscopes so we could look at some cells and other tiny things.

Ms. Langley's eyes fastened on the loudest giggler—Lucy—like a low-flying hawk fastening on a rat. The giggles stopped dead. Ms. Langley stepped into the room and spotted Mr. In, who had looked up from his work to see who was at the door.

"Excuse me, Mr. In," she said. She sounded a little too sweet, like somebody who doesn't really feel like being sweet. "I'd just like to observe for a few minutes."

"Of course," Mr. In said. "There's an extra chair by the window if you'd like to sit down."

A few minutes later we took turns going to the back of the room to look through the microscopes. I forgot all about Ms. Langley being there until I was on my way back to my seat, and then I noticed her writing in a small green notebook. What's she writing? I wondered.

Then Brian Laidlaw had one of his weird moments. I guess he didn't like the ant farm—a big one that sat on a table near the last of the microscopes. Maybe the ants creeped him out. Because just as I sat down, I heard his voice, and it was loud and nervous: "I hate ants."

"Just ignore them, Brian," Mr. In said quietly. "You have one microscope left—just look in and then answer the question on your paper."

"No." He shook his head hard. "No. No, no, no!" His voice got louder with each "no," and the whole class was staring.

"Would you like for me to move the ant farm to another table?" Mr. In asked calmly. He was standing in the back near the microscopes, and his voice was so soft I could hardly hear him. We'd seen him calm down Brian before, but this time he was too late. Brian was already losing it.

"I *hate* ants! I *hate* ants!" Brian's fists were clenched and his legs were twitching.

"OK, Brian," Mr. In said, "you can—" But I didn't hear the rest of his sentence, because Kyle started humming.

I couldn't believe it. Most of us were dead quiet, just watching Brian and wondering what would happen next. And *Ms. Langley* was in the room, with her hawk eyes roving around. But Kyle, sitting next to me, must have thought the whole thing was funny. The tune he was humming was unmistakable, and everybody knew the words: "The ants go marching one by one, hurrah, hurrah . . ."

James, who was right behind me, joined in, raising the volume. Other people started looking around, wondering who was humming.

Brian Laidlaw froze and went silent.

There was a long moment when nobody said a word, and the only sound was the humming of the ant song. And then Brian whirled around to face the class and yelled, "Stop it!" He ran out of the room, with Mr. In dashing after him.

Everybody started chattering and laughing—for about three seconds, till Ms. Langley got up from her chair, stalked to the front of the class, and ordered us all to be quiet.

We did.

She kept on standing in front of us, but she started scribbling in her little notebook again.

· · · · ·

We had recess right after that. A bunch of us, bundled up against the cold, stood by the monkey bars talking about Brian and Ms. Langley.

"I didn't know Brian was scared of ants," Deena said.

"He's scared of all kinds of bugs," Charity answered. "Remember that field trip when we went to the park and people found cicadas?"

"Yeah, that really freaked him out," Adam said. He jumped up to grab the monkey bars and swung himself across. We all watched, because he could cross the monkey bars faster than anybody. Dropping off the other end, he added, "That and fire drills, noisy crowds, snare drums, cymbals, dogs, hyenas, wildebeests, bunny rabbits . . ."

I laughed, but I kind of felt sorry for Brian too. Then a new idea hit me. "Hey, maybe he's scared of Ms. Langley. Maybe she makes him nervous, and that's why he got so freaked out about the ants. They've been there for two weeks, and he never screamed about them before."

"Ms. Langley scares everybody," Deena said. "Even teachers. Ms. Day used to get all nervous every time Ms. Langley came in our room."

I'd been in the other fourth-grade class, so I didn't know about that. "Why did she come in your class? Mr. Evans never did when he was principal."

"I don't know," Deena said, "but near the end of the year she used to come in all the time and take notes, just like she was doing today. I think she didn't like Ms. Day, and that's why Ms. Day didn't come back this year."

"You mean, like, she was writing down that

Ms. Day was a bad teacher or something?" Adam asked. "And then she fired her?"

"Probably," Deena said. "You could see Ms. Day turn white the minute Ms. Langley walked in. And now Ms. Day is gone."

Charity's voice was hushed. "She couldn't do that to Mr. In—could she?"

There was silence for a moment.

"No way," I said. "He's a really good teacher."

"But if she doesn't like him," Adam said, "she could fire him. She's his boss."

"She'd have to be crazy to fire him," Charity argued.

"Maybe she *is* crazy," I said, remembering how she'd gotten way more upset when I shoved Kyle a little than when I beat up Leo.

"Well," Deena said hopefully, "she's only come to Mr. In's class once."

"Twice," Adam and I said at the same time.

"Weren't you there last Friday, when she watched our math lesson?" Adam said.

"I don't—oh, that was probably when I went to the dentist," Deena said. "She's been here twice?"

The rest of us nodded.

Deena shook her head. "That's not good."

. . . . .

After a few days of Brian fiddling around, doing almost nothing to help me get our project going, I decided to talk to Mr. In. I hung around after the last bell, while everyone else left. Mr. In was sitting behind his desk, watching me with his eyebrows raised. I told him Brian wasn't doing anything, and I didn't see how we were going to do this project together.

"It's just not working," I said. "Can't I get a new partner or something? Or just do my own project on Australia and let Brian do one by himself?"

Mr. In looked thoughtful. "I know it's not easy to work with Brian. Social studies is hard for him, and so is this kind of cooperative project. But I think you might be the very best person in this class for him to work with—the person who can bring out his best effort."

"Me?" I stared at his smooth brown face. This wasn't the kind of answer I'd expected at all. Did he think I could work with Brian because I was weird too?

"I've noticed that you have empathy for people who are different, Sylvan. You don't ridicule them or ignore them the way some students do. You're curious about other people and places, and you always give people a chance. That makes Brian more comfortable with you than he is with some of the other kids."

"Maybe," I said slowly. The compliment surprised me. I had an uneasy feeling that I didn't deserve it. And anyway, it didn't solve the problem. "But he doesn't want to find out anything about Australia. All he wants to do is math games."

Mr. In smiled. "Yes, I know. But that can be part of the solution. We'll play to Brian's strengths."

I didn't understand what he meant at first. But Mr. In is a very smart guy.

· · · · ·

When Will picked me up after work on Friday, he was a little late, and I had my jacket on and my backpack ready to go. I was trying to get Zachary to jump up and grab a crow feather that I was twirling over his head when I heard Will's knock. I dropped the feather and ran to the door.

Will was wearing his favorite gray jacket that has silver triangles all over it to reflect light. It's mostly for biking or running at night. It's a really cool jacket.

"Hey there, stretch," he said. "Did you grow a foot this week?"

"No, you shrank a foot."

"OK, wise guy, that's it." He practically jumped through the doorway, then grabbed me and turned me upside down for a second before setting my feet on the floor again.

As soon as I was right side up I saw that Lila had come out of the kitchen, and she was actually smiling just the tiniest bit. This was pretty good. Some Fridays when Will comes, she doesn't go near the door—just yells "bye" to me from whatever room she's in.

Will was panting a little. "You're getting too heavy." Then he looked over at her. "Hi, how's it going?"

"Not bad." She had a pen in her hand and was clicking it so the point went in and out. "Listen, you want some eggs? Josephine and Zsa Zsa are on a roll this week."

"Sure, I'll take a few."

She went to the kitchen and returned with a carton.

"Thanks. Sylvan, you ready to go?"

"Sure." We both said good-bye to Lila and started out the door.

"Backpack, Sylvan," Lila called.

I went back and got it. She gave me a fast hug, and then I ran out to the car.

It was a good way to start the weekend, with Will and Lila being almost friendly. I didn't have to feel bad about leaving Lila by herself.

Justin told me a long time ago that parents who separate almost never get back together. "Don't even hope for it," he said. "It's not going to happen."

But sometimes I did hope, a little.

· · · · ·

At the end of school one day in December, I was pushing between puffy coats and backpacks toward the doors. Behind me, Charity yelled, "Sylvan, guess what?"

"What?"

"We got a dog! Do you want to come over and see him?"

I paused. I never hung around with girls.

"What kind?" I asked her as we squeezed through the front door and into the cold air.

"He's a mix. Part Lab, I think. That's what Mom says, anyway."

"Cool." I really wanted to see the dog. "OK, but first I have to go home and ask my mom. Then maybe I can come over after that."

I ran all the way home, and Lila said OK, so I got a snack and then walked over.

Mr. Jensen wasn't around, which was cool with me. He made me a little nervous. He'd never said anything mean to me or even around me, but he had this fierce look. He seemed like a guy who could get mad fast. Pastors weren't supposed to be like that, I thought. But I didn't know many pastors. Lila and I never went to church.

Faith and Charity couldn't wait to show me the dog. It was out in their fenced-in backyard, barking at a squirrel in a tree. As soon as we stepped out the door, the dog bounded forward and did a kind of dance around us, like he couldn't decide which one of us to jump on first.

He was big and yellowish brown, with short hair, a wide nose, and a big toothy grin. Faith captured him by throwing her arms around his neck, and he licked her face enthusiastically.

"His name's JJ," Charity said, patting him. "And he loves every single person he sees."

"He's great," I said. I was kind of jealous. I liked Zachary and the chickens, but it would be nice to have a dog too. The trouble was, Lila didn't like dogs. Maybe I could talk Will into getting one.

"Come on, JJ," Charity said. "Show Sylvan how you can fetch." She picked up a tennis ball and threw it, and JJ raced after it.

When he came back, he dropped the ball in front of us, and I grabbed it. It was all slobbery, but I didn't mind. I threw it hard—a lot farther than Charity could throw—and JJ took off again.

I had just thrown the ball for about the tenth time when I heard people talking and looked around. On the sidewalk at the end of Charity's driveway I saw Lucy and Melissa, just standing there and looking at us. Lucy waved when she saw me looking. I waved back, and then Charity and Faith saw them too.

"There's that girl from your class," Faith said.

Charity just nodded. She didn't look thrilled.

Lucy and Melissa were talking back and forth, too quietly for us to hear, and then Melissa said, louder, "Come on, I want to see it," and both girls walked down the driveway toward us, Lucy hanging back a little.

"Can we see your dog?" Melissa asked as they came up to the gate.

"OK," Charity said. Melissa and Lucy came in and petted JJ, while Charity told them about going to the animal shelter and picking him out.

Melissa kept petting JJ, and she asked a couple of questions. But Lucy stood off to the side and kept twirling her finger in her curly hair and looking bored. Finally, she nudged Melissa and tugged on her arm. "OK," Melissa said, interrupting Charity in the middle of a sentence. "I guess we're gonna go now." They both said goodbye and left, shoulders bumping against each other as they walked away.

"They're not very nice," Charity muttered.

"Yeah, I know," I said.

"They wouldn't have even said hi, except Melissa wanted to see JJ."

The dog flopped down to rest, chewing on the ball. Faith cartwheeled across the yard.

Charity stared at JJ, but I don't think she was seeing him. "They think I'm weird," she said, and for a second I was afraid she was going to start crying.

"You're not weird," I said quickly, even though I thought she kind of was. But not as weird as I'd thought the first week of school.

I wouldn't care if Melissa and Lucy were rude to *me*, but Charity probably didn't have any real friends in the whole town.

She looked at me with big eyes, as if she wanted help. "Everything was different in Kenya—I had *lots* of friends. Here everybody just thinks I'm the weird new kid."

I thought about that. "Well, you were a new kid when you first went to Kenya, weren't you? I mean, you came from a foreign country and your skin was white and you only spoke English, right? But you made friends anyway."

She nodded sadly.

"So why can't you do the same thing here?"

"I don't know. I was only five when we went there. I guess it's different when you're little—you just do things. You don't think about them."

I could understand that. It seemed sort of like the way everything was different when I was little, and Lila and Will and me and Justin were still together. That's your world, and it's so right and so normal you never even think about it. Then it falls apart.

chapter eight

CHARITY

When Dad said he didn't believe anymore, it was like the whole world turned upside down. This could not be happening. It just couldn't.

How could Dad *not* believe? God was real. God was true. Jesus was our savior. I knew these things because—because Dad and Mom had always said so. And Dad was a *pastor*—the one who helped other people to believe. How could my father, my big strong father who everyone respected, fall into this terrible mistake?

For maybe half a minute, I wondered if Dad could possibly be right—right *this* time, I mean, and wrong all the years before. I wondered if it was possible that religion was all a big mistake, just something people wanted to believe in. But that was a thought so weird and scary that I put it out of my mind immediately. Mom still believed, and millions of other people did too. They couldn't all be wrong.

Dad is going to be all right, I told myself over and over during those last few weeks in Kenya. He'll start believing again someday. He'll find a church in America and go back to being a pastor. Then he'll smile and laugh again, and we'll call him Bwana Simba just to tease him.

But during those weeks nobody dared to tease him. And he never smiled or laughed.

. . . . .

In America Mom took me and Faith to church every Sunday, and almost every Sunday Faith wanted to know why Dad wasn't going with us.

"We *told* you already," I said.

Mom explained patiently, again, that Dad was

very sad and disappointed about how things had turned out in Kenya—about Mr. Kafuna and the spire and the way fewer and fewer people came to church. He was so sad that he wasn't sure God loved him anymore. But God did love him and all of us, Mom assured Faith. Someday Dad would realize that and come back to church.

I wondered if she really believed Dad would do that. I believed it at first—during the month with Grandma and Grandpa, and then for the first few weeks in our new house. Everything was new and all mixed up, and I thought after we settled in, Dad would be his old self again.

But as more and more weeks went by, I wasn't so sure. Dad didn't ever pray, as far as I could tell, and when the rest of us went to church, he stayed home and did chores or read books.

Then he got a job painting houses, and that seemed to make him feel a little better. It was getting too cold for outside work, he said, but the company had a lot of indoor painting jobs. He came home every night in his paint-spattered clothes and took a long shower before dinner.

He wasn't like his old self, though. He was quiet, and he didn't seem so strong anymore.

· · · · ·

At school I was usually too busy to worry about Dad. For one thing, the social studies project looked like fun. I picked India as my first choice, mainly because I remembered seeing a lot of Indians in the cities in Kenya—in Nairobi and Kisumu and Mombasa. Some of the women wore beautiful saris—long pieces of cloth wrapped around their waists and over their shoulders. I was ready to learn all kinds of things about Indians, like all about their strange religion and why so many of them are poor. Maybe I'd find out why so many Indians moved to Kenya.

But then Mr. In made me partners with *Adam*—probably my least favorite person in the whole class. He was never friendly at all, and sometimes he called me Preacher Girl. I looked at him when Mr. In announced that we got India, and he was rolling his eyes, like "oh, no, I'm stuck with *Charity*." Well, I wanted to say, for your information, Adam Gardner, that's exactly how I feel about being stuck with *you*.

Deena sits next to me, and she says he's cute. She likes his big brown eyes and long eyelashes. But I say you can't be a jerk and cute at the same time, no matter how long your eyelashes are.

As soon as we started the projects, I put together a list of topics—all the things Mr. In had said every team had to cover, like the kind of government, climate, geography—plus a few other things, like the kinds of clothing and the caste system that divides people into separate groups. I handed the list to Adam, but he barely glanced at it before dropping it on his desk. He was doodling, and talking to Peter, and fidgeting, but he wasn't listening to me.

I had already checked off the topics I was most interested in, but I wasn't telling him he had to do everything else. I was just trying to get him to say which topics he wanted, so if we wanted the same ones, we could make trades, and each of us would end up with half the list.

The longer he ignored me and messed around, the madder I got.

"Adam, come *on*," I said. "We have to *do* this."

"Oh, all right," he grumbled. He picked up the list and gave it a brief, bored look. "You left out snake charmers," he said and handed it back.

"Snake charmers?"

"Yeah. I want to know if they're for real."

"They're not," I said. "That's just a myth."

"How do *you* know?"

"Think about it!" I said impatiently. "How could playing a little music make a snake come dancing out of a basket?"

"Inquiring minds want to know," he said solemnly. "That will be my quest—to discover the truth about snake charmers."

"What about all the other topics?"

"Later." He yawned and stretched, looking up at the ceiling. "When I finish my quest, I might be able to look into a couple of those."

I was ready to scream. "I'm going to tell Mr. In you're not helping," I hissed at him.

That got his attention, and for once he looked me in the eye.

"Nobody likes a tattletale."

For a minute I was speechless, and I felt my face getting hotter. It was as if he knew, somehow just knew, how bad I felt about not making a lot of friends. It was like he'd found the one sore spot on my arm and poked it with a big sharp needle.

I felt the sting of angry, frustrated tears in my eyes, and blinked them back.

"Fine!" I said to Adam. "*Do* snake charmers!" I was so fed up with him I could hardly get the words out. "But there's more to India than snake charmers!"

"Charity, try to keep your voice down," Mr. In said mildly. Adam leaned back, crossed his arms, and smirked.

$$\cdot \ \cdot \ \cdot \ \cdot \ \cdot$$

At night it took me a long time to fall asleep. I kept thinking about how some of the kids said Ms. Langley wanted to fire Mr. In. And the more I thought about it, the more I was convinced it was true. I kept going over in my mind everything I'd heard about the principal, especially

Deena saying how she took notes in Ms. Day's class and Ms. Day looked upset and the next fall Ms. Day was gone.

And it wasn't just Deena—other kids said bad things about Ms. Langley too. They said she wasn't fair. They said that she suspended kids for practically nothing and that one day she'd be nice, but the next day she'd yell at kids for the littlest thing. Sylvan said he and another kid were just shoving each other a little and she got furious, but when he did something a lot worse, she was perfectly calm. That doesn't make any sense at all.

I almost asked Sylvan what the bad thing he did was. But he looked so upset when he said it that I didn't.

If the principal turned against Mr. In . . . she could fire him and he'd have to leave. Maybe he wouldn't even get to finish the year. What if we came back from Christmas vacation and found a stranger in our classroom?

Just thinking about it made me really angry. Mr. In was such a great teacher. If he got pushed out, that would be the most unfair thing in the world.

I thought about how kind he was, how he'd understood why I didn't act like everyone else in the class. He made me feel good about school, even though I had trouble fitting in. Even if I didn't know what to do with the other kids sometimes, with Mr. In I always felt good—like he thought I was interesting and smart and not weird at all.

The idea of losing Mr. In didn't just make me angry. It also made me scared. It gave me a hollow feeling in my stomach. Like I was counting on Mr. In to be there, and if he wasn't, I'd be lost—the way I'd once been lost, when I was little, in a field of sugarcane. The plants were too tall to see over. They seemed to go on forever in every direction, and the wind in the leaves confused all the other sounds.

My father had changed into someone I couldn't count on anymore, someone I hardly recognized. I would do anything to keep Mr. In from disappearing too. But what could I do?

· · · · ·

Ms. Langley came back a few days later. She sat through half of a science lesson about biomes, and I couldn't concentrate on the tundra and the rain forest and all those other places because I kept looking over at her, sitting in the chair by the window, to see what she was doing.

Sometimes she would turn her head slowly, looking over the whole classroom, half smiling. I didn't trust that half smile at all. Ms. Langley smiled like a crocodile. Other times she had the hawk look, zeroing in on somebody. With so many of us in the room, it was hard to tell which kid she was staring at. But when she looked to the front of the room with those sharp hawk eyes, there was only one target: Mr. In. Often, after staring at him, she wrote something in her green notebook.

When she left the room, it was like a dark cloud had drifted away.

Two days later, a man with a big bald circle on top of his head took the chair by the window. He stayed there during morning meeting and all through the math and spelling lessons after it. Mr. In said only that he was "a visitor" who wanted to see what our class was like. Whoever he was, the bald man didn't look like a teacher. He was all dressed up in a dark blue suit and a blue and gray tie. He stayed longer than Ms. Langley ever did, and he had a notebook too, a big black one. He wrote a lot in it, so much that it was hard to believe he was paying attention to our class at all.

Later, when we were outside for recess, I saw him standing around on the edge of the playground with his hands in the pockets of his overcoat. I wondered if his bald head was cold, and I wondered if he was judging Mr. In by the way we behaved on the playground. Then Ms. Langley came outside too, and they stood there talking to each other. I dropped out of the kickball game and circled around behind them, hoping to hear what they were saying.

It was a windy day, the breeze pushing at bare twigs on the trees outside the playground fence. Ms. Langley pulled a scarf up around her chin as she listened to the stranger. As I got closer I stopped looking at them and pretended to be looking for something on the ground.

I caught a few words here and there. "Not fully prepared ... poor environment ... limitations ..."

There was a pause in the conversation, and then I heard that sharp-sweet voice. "Have you lost something, Charity?"

I looked up at her as innocently as I could. "Um, I think I dropped a nickel over here."

She smiled her crocodile half-smile. "Well, good luck finding it."

And she and the stranger walked off a little way, stopping to talk again near the school door.

For the rest of recess I sat on a swing and worried about Mr. In. He was "not fully prepared." He had "limitations." His class had a "poor environment." If that's what the old crocodile and the stranger thought of Mr. In, how long could we possibly keep him?

· · · · ·

I told Deena what I'd heard, and Deena told everybody to meet by the swings at recess the next day.

158

The whole class gathered there as soon as we got outside. Even Brian, who started to wander off toward the climbing bars, seemed to suddenly notice what was happening. He came over too and stood at the back of the group. Deena and I stood on one of the railroad ties that kept the wood chips piled up around the swings, so we were a little taller than the rest.

"Listen, everybody," Deena said. "Charity heard something about Mr. In. Tell them, Charity."

So, with everybody's eyes on me, I took a deep breath and told them about the stranger and Ms. Langley and the things they'd said. Every single person was listening, even more than the day I'd told them about living in Kenya. Even girls like Melissa and Lucy, who always ignored me. And even though I was worried about Mr. In, I felt good because of that.

"She wants to fire him," Deena said angrily as soon as I finished. "Just like Ms. Day."

Some of the kids were nodding.

"She hated Ms. Day," Peter said. "You could tell."

"She kept coming to class and writing things in her notebook," Eli added. "Just like she's been doing with Mr. In."

"But who's that man, the one that came yesterday? What does he have to do with it?" Adam asked.

"Yeah, does anybody know who he is?" Sylvan chimed in.

We all just looked at one another. Nobody had an answer.

"Ms. Langley is so mean, she probably does want to fire Mr. In," Melissa said. "But what can we do about it?"

More silence. Then Sylvan said, "What we need is a petition, and everybody in the whole class has to sign it."

Deena's face lit up. "Yeah, a petition! That's a great idea. We could get other kids to sign it too—not just our class."

I didn't understand. I'd never heard of a petition. Was this another thing that every American kid knew, except me? I didn't want to be the weird one again, so I kept quiet.

But Lucy asked the question for me. "What's a petition?"

"It's sort of like a letter," Sylvan answered. "You write down what you want to happen, and you get as many people as you can to sign it. So we'd write something about how great Mr. In is and how we want him to stay."

"Then what do we do with it?" Lucy said.

"Give it to Ms. Langley," Melissa said, pushing back her hair as the wind blew it over her eyes.

"No, give it to the superintendent," Adam said. "He's her boss. He's the boss of all the schools in the whole county."

"Yeah," Sylvan said. "My mom's always doing things like this, and she says you have to go to the top."

Everyone was nodding and agreeing, so Deena said, "OK, how about Sylvan and Charity write it tonight and bring it in tomorrow? Because Sylvan knows about petitions, and Charity heard what Ms. Langley and that man said."

I looked at Sylvan, and we both said, "OK."

"But it has to be a secret," Melissa said. "We don't want Ms. Langley to see it. She'd probably take it away or something."

"What about Mr. In?" Lucy said. "Should we tell him we're doing this?"

Some people said yes, some said no, and some just shrugged. But then Adam said something really smart, something I hadn't thought of.

"We can't tell him," Adam said. "Because we don't want the superintendent to think Mr. In made us do this. So it's better if we can say he doesn't know, and then if the superintendent tells him, he can be totally surprised."

"Yeah, cool," Sylvan said. "But who *is* the superintendent, anyway?"

"I think his name's Mr. Borthwick," Melissa said.

"I can find out," Adam said. "My dad has the school website bookmarked on his computer. I'll check and call Sylvan tonight."

"Get the address too," Sylvan said.

· · · · ·

That afternoon, as soon as Mom got home from the hospital, I told her that I had a homework project to do with Sylvan. I didn't want to say what we were really doing. If she asked what the homework was, I was going to say we had to write letters, but she didn't even ask. She just said this would be a great day to invite Sylvan and his mother to come for dinner, and right away she picked up the phone.

chapter nine

SYLVAN

I didn't want to go to Charity's for dinner. I figured we could write the petition in twenty minutes at one house or the other, and I wasn't interested in spending extra time with Charity. Dinner with parents would probably take hours.

But when Mrs. Jensen called to invite us, Lila accepted without even asking me what I thought.

I dragged my feet, hoping that unlike us, the Jensens might have a TV, and we could watch a movie or something after we finished the petition. So as soon as the Jensens opened the door and led us into their living room, I looked all around, but there was no TV in sight. The room was almost bare. At our house, there's stuff everywhere, but in Charity's living room, there was a couch, a big armchair, a coffee table, and one small, half-empty bookcase. No rug, no pictures on the walls, no lamps—just one light in the ceiling. No magazines or flower vases or family photos.

"I'm running a little late," Mrs. Jensen said, "so dinner won't be ready for a while. Charity, you and Sylvan should get your homework done before dinner."

"Anything I can help with?" Lila asked.

"Why don't you just come in the kitchen and keep me company?" Mrs. Jensen said. "Faith, you set the table, and then you can play, but don't bother Charity and Sylvan while they're doing homework."

"*Ohh*-kaay," Faith said, stretching the word out in a complaining voice. She followed the moms into the kitchen.

"I'll get some paper," Charity said and disappeared.

Mr. Jensen stood in the doorway. "So you and Charity have homework to do together?"

"Um, yeah." I felt kind of awkward, with nothing to do except look at him, this powerful-looking man in a plaid shirt. He stood there with a face that was kind of friendly but somehow made me nervous. I hoped he wasn't going to ask me what the homework was, because I wasn't sure I wanted to tell any grown-ups about it.

"What's the homework?" he asked.

"Um—"

"We have to write letters," Charity put in quickly, coming up beside him. "Persuasive letters—that's what Mr. In calls them. We're supposed to figure out how to convince someone to agree with us." She sounded smooth as soft ice cream, and I was impressed. I'd never have expected Charity to be a good liar.

"Hmm," Mr. Jensen said. "What's the point you're trying to get across?"

Even this didn't trip her up. "Oh, he gave us

three or four topics. We have to decide which one to work on."

She laid a few pieces of paper and a pen on the coffee table. Just then, Mrs. Jensen called from the kitchen, "Martin, can you open this jar?"

"On my way," he said and went to the kitchen, where Lila started talking to him. I figured he wouldn't be back for a while.

"Wow," I whispered to Charity. "You're a good liar."

She looked insulted. "I was *not* lying. Not much, anyway. A petition *is* a persuasive letter."

"If you say so."

"Well, how do we start?" she asked.

"Oh," I said, pulling a piece of paper from my jeans pocket. "I've got the name and address— Adam told me."

I smoothed the paper out on the table and picked up a pen. "Wait," Charity said. "Do you have good handwriting?"

"Um, not really. That paragraph we turned in yesterday—Mr. In said it looked like our chickens scratched on it with ink on their feet."

Charity giggled. "Well, maybe I should write it. You tell me what to say."

I'd seen more petitions than any kid in the class—that was for sure. Lila was always writing one or signing one, online or on paper, and sometimes she showed them to me. "Look at this," she'd say. "It's a petition to the state Department of Conservation, asking them to investigate the chemicals in the river near Watsonville. See how many people have signed it? And that's just in our neighborhood. We're going to combine all these papers and count up the signatures. We've got hundreds and hundreds of people on our side."

I could have asked Lila for advice on writing our petition, but I didn't want to. I wanted us to do it ourselves, without any grown-ups getting involved. So I started talking, and Charity started writing.

Dear Mr. Borthwick,
We are students at Henderson Elementary. We want to tell you about our great teacher, Mr. In.

Charity looked up. "I think we should write his whole name, not just 'Mr. In.'"

"Sure," I said. "I guess, but I don't know how to spell it."

"I do."

That didn't exactly surprise me.

The next few sentences were harder. I knew we needed to say *why* Mr. In was a great teacher, but I didn't know how to put it. Charity had some ideas, though, and we talked our way through the rest of the petition. It ended up like this:

Dear Mr. Borthwick,

We are students at Henderson Elementary. We want to tell you about our great teacher, Mr. Inayatullah. He's really smart and he gives us interesting projects to work on together, like the one we're doing right now about different countries around the world. He's nice to everyone in the class and he really understands us and helps us get along with each other. We are learning a lot every day.

Please don't listen to anyone who says he shouldn't teach here. We want to have Mr. Inayatullah for our teacher all year, and we want him to stay at Henderson forever. Or maybe teach at the middle school so we can have him again next year.

Sincerely,

Charity and I read it over silently. "It's good," she said.

"Yeah. And tomorrow we'll get everybody to sign it—the whole class."

When we went into the dining room, there was a platter of chicken in the middle of the table. Mrs. Jensen turned to me right away, looking a little upset. "Sylvan, I'm so sorry about the chicken. Your mother just told me that you're vegetarians. I really should have asked before I made dinner, and I just didn't think of it."

"That's OK," I said.

"Debbie, please!" Lila said, smiling. "It's no big deal. We don't mind."

"Well, I hope you have enough to eat," Mrs. Jensen said.

"Don't be silly—I see rice and vegetables and this beautiful salad, and I've been craving some greens all day. We're fine."

I was hungry, and the chicken smelled really good, until I reminded myself that it had once been a living creature like Zsa Zsa.

Everyone sat down, and Mrs. Jensen said, "Let's take a moment to say grace." Faith and Charity and Mrs. Jensen bowed their heads and closed their eyes. Lila sat with her hands in her lap, looking down at her plate, so I did too. But I raised my eyes for a second, just long enough to see that Mr. Jensen was staring into space. He wasn't even *trying* to look like he was saying grace.

Mrs. Jensen said some things about being thankful for good food and friends, and we all began to eat.

Dinner ended with apple pie and vanilla ice cream, one of my favorite things in the world. The pie was from a store and not as good as Lila's homemade pie, but I still ate a big piece.

As we took our dessert plates into the kitchen, Faith poked my arm. "Want to see my room?"

She was looking up at me with her big blue eyes, and her curly hair was tied with green ribbons.

"Umm . . ."

"He doesn't care about girls' rooms, Faith," Charity said impatiently. "Let's play a board game."

"I want him to see my horses," Faith insisted.

She was so little she didn't even come up to my shoulder. She was a midget compared to me. And suddenly I remembered Justin calling me "midget," and how I always wanted to show him things, but most of the time he wasn't interested.

"OK," I said. "Let's go see your room."

Faith skipped off down the hall, and Charity and I followed.

I looked at Faith's plastic horses, her dolls, the pink flowered curtains on her window, and her quilt with ponies on it, and I said they were all great, trying to sound like I meant it. Then Faith led the way into Charity's room. She seemed to want me to see it a lot more than Charity did.

It wasn't like any other kid's room that I'd ever seen. No posters on the walls; no dresser like most girls had, with a top all covered with beads and nail polish and hairbrushes; and no furry pile of stuffed animals on the bed. Charity's room was all about Africa.

A cloth with a deep green and sunflower yellow pattern covered her bed. Along the edge there were words in another language—Swahili, Faith told me. On her bookshelves were baskets, wooden cups, and three small stone figures—a rhinoceros, a hippopotamus, and a giraffe. On the walls were cloths with African people painted on them, and pictures of African scenes that were made of wood and (Charity told me) banana tree fibers. There were photos too, like the ones Charity had brought to school—pictures of her African school, her house, the church, her friends.

"Cool," I said softly. It was like walking into another world.

I wished I'd had the chance to go somewhere far away, instead of always living right here. I wished I knew all about another country and could speak a different language.

Then I realized something: I hadn't seen a single African basket or picture or anything in any room in the house except Charity's. The rest of their house looked like any other American house, except kind of bare. I asked her why.

Charity hesitated for half a second, and Faith spoke up ahead of her. "Because Daddy hates African things," she said, bouncing as she sat on Charity's bed. "He doesn't want to see any of this stuff."

"Then why does he let you cover your whole room with it?" I asked.

"Mom and Dad said we could decorate our rooms however we wanted to," Charity said. "I guess he never thought I'd want these things. He'd already told Mom he couldn't stand having them in the rest of the house. So he doesn't like it, but he couldn't go back on his word."

Faith piped up again. "Every time he walks by, he closes the door."

"But I don't care," Charity said stubbornly. "I like these things. I liked living in Kenya."

Looking at her face, I thought she was going to add "a lot better than here." But she didn't.

"Didn't your dad like it there?"

"He used to. At first," Charity said slowly. She seemed to be deciding whether she really wanted to explain or not.

And then she told me the story of the church in Kenya and how some of the people didn't like her father and how he wanted more than anything to build the spire. And then the man fell off the roof and died. And now Mr. Jensen didn't even believe in God.

I went home thinking that amazing things had happened to Charity Jensen.

· · · · ·

That night I typed the petition on Lila's computer and printed it out. Charity and I had decided it would look more serious that way. The next day I went to school early and got some kids to sign it before the first bell. At recess Charity and I asked everybody else in our class and some of the kids in the other fifth grade too. The more names the better, we figured.

Finally, we stood in a group—Charity, Deena, Adam, and me—and looked over the petition. It was wrinkled from all the handling, but it still looked pretty impressive, I thought.

"We should make sure every single person in our class signed it," Deena said. "Let's count."

Each of us counted, lips moving silently or in a whisper, fingers jabbing at the names, skipping over the ones from the other class. All of us came up with twenty-one, but we knew our class had twenty-two.

"Who are we missing?" Deena asked.

A few seconds of silence.

"I know," Adam said. "The Trampoline Kid."

We all looked around. To find Brian, you didn't need to look at groups of kids playing kickball or dodgeball. You needed to look in the corners of the playground, in small spaces, and you needed to look for one kid completely alone.

"There," Charity said. "By the slide."

Brian was running his hands down the surface of the slide, maybe feeling how smooth it was. The four of us hurried across the playground.

"Brian," I called as we approached him. "We need you to sign this."

He looked at us curiously, and his hands tightened on the slide's edge.

"It's the petition, remember?" I said. "So they won't fire Mr. In." I put the paper on the slide in front of him and held out a pen.

Brian took the pen and stared at the petition.

Adam started drumming his fingers on the slide. "Come on, Brian, just write your name at the bottom."

"Give him time to read it," Charity said.

"OK, Preacher Girl."

"That is not my name!"

I thought it was important for every single kid in the class to sign this petition—to show that we were all together on this. So I really wanted Brian to sign. Why was he hesitating? I couldn't think of anything he could have against Mr. In. Maybe he hadn't been paying attention when we talked about it the day before, or maybe he just couldn't think with all four of us staring at him and Adam and Charity snapping at each other.

I grabbed Adam's arm to distract him from baiting Charity. "You guys go somewhere else. Let me talk to Brian."

"Sylvan's right," Deena said. "Come on."

When they had moved off, I turned to Brian. "So, OK, remember yesterday at recess we talked about how Ms. Langley doesn't like Mr. In, and we're afraid she might fire him? So he wouldn't be our teacher anymore?"

Brian nodded without looking at me.

"So we want everybody to sign this petition, and then we'll send it to Mr. Borthwick, because he's Ms. Langley's boss. And if she tries to fire Mr. In, Mr. Borthwick will know that's crazy because we all say Mr. In is great. And then he won't let her fire him."

Brian nodded again.

"So could you please write your name on it?"

Brian signed his name in big cursive letters,

very carefully. "Mr. In is nice," he said. "I like Mr. In."

"Yeah, Mr. In rocks."

I picked up the petition. Brian was looking all around, twiddling the pen in his fingers, moving it from one hand to the other. I stood there a little longer.

"Can I have the pen back?" I said.

. . . . .

We mailed the petition to Mr. Borthwick at the district office, with thirty-seven names on it. Then we waited.

Meanwhile, we were working hard on our social studies projects. In about a week each team would have to present their country to the whole class. Mr. In said we'd be graded on our posters, our written reports, and how well we gave our presentations. We'd heard all that before. But then he added something new.

"We'll have two or three visitors, including Ms. Langley, on presentation day, so I hope you'll all show them what a great job you can do."

Adam and I looked at each other. I wondered if my eyes were as wide as his. I glanced around the room and saw that Charity's face was all serious and Deena looked nervous.

"Nothing to worry about, though," Mr. In said with a smile. "I'm impressed with your progress so far."

· · · · ·

The next day at lunch I asked Adam if he wanted to hang out after school, but he gulped down the last piece of his PB&J and said he couldn't.

"Why not?"

"My cousin's coming over. You know, Kevin."

Kevin was three years older than us and played lacrosse. He didn't live close to us, but sometimes I saw him riding his bike to the middle school.

"Maybe he'd play soccer with us," I said, hoping Adam would tell me to come on over too.

"Not today," he said, stuffing plastic bags back into his lunchbox. "He's bringing me something to use for the India thing."

"What's he bringing?"

Adam grinned. "Can't tell you. It's gonna be a surprise."

He didn't usually keep secrets from me. I didn't like it. "Just tell me—I won't tell anybody."

For a second he looked like he wanted to, like this secret was so big it was about to burst out of him. But he shook his head with another big grin. "Sorry, Tree Boy. I better not. But I promise, you're gonna love it."

At the end of the day, as soon as we got outside, he said, "See you tomorrow," and took off running.

. . . . .

A couple of days later, Charity caught up with me as I was walking home from school. It was Wednesday, and Friday was presentation day. Adam had his piano lesson, so I was by myself. The afternoon was cold and gray, and the clouds looked like wet cement.

"I hope all the presentations turn out to be good," Charity said. "If they don't, Ms. Langley will think it's Mr. In's fault."

"I know."

"Is yours going to be OK? I mean, Brian—?"

"Yeah, he's doing OK. He did part of the report, and he's making his own poster. But I don't know if he can talk in front of the class. He's always so nervous. I mean, what if he just stands there and won't say a word? Or freaks out and does something weird?"

"Ugh," Charity said. "That would be awful."

We were silent for a block.

Then Charity said, "I'm not too sure about Adam, either. He's acting strange. I think he has some secret plan." She looked at me sharply. "Did he tell you what he's going to do?"

"No."

"He didn't say he has a surprise for presentation day or something like that?"

I hesitated. Telling Charity what Adam had said seemed wrong, even though he hadn't let me in on the secret. "Umm, not really."

She gave me a disbelieving look.

"I swear, he didn't tell me he was going to do anything." That was true, sort of.

"Well," she said, "Mr. In told him if he wanted

to do snake charmers, he had to explain Indian religion and culture, and say how snake charmers fit into all that. But he looks too happy about it. I think he's up to something."

"I don't know, but Adam's pretty smart, and he can talk in front of a class, you know? Whatever he does, it won't be a problem for Mr. In."

"I hope you're right," Charity said doubtfully. I hoped I was too.

. . . . .

That night after dinner Charity called me. "I have an idea," she said, breathing fast.

"What?"

"Well, nobody knows what Brian might do when you guys do your presentation, right?"

"Yeah."

"And if he does something crazy or even if he just stands there mumbling, it'll make Mr. In look bad in front of Ms. Langley."

"Yeah, but—"

"So we have to get Brian to practice. Tomorrow after school. You and Brian can do the presentation, and I'll be the audience."

"Um, I don't know," I muttered. Use up my free time working with Brian? "I was planning to do something with Adam tomorrow."

"This is *important*," Charity said. "You can do things with Adam anytime. We have to do everything we can to save Mr. In, and we only have a couple days left."

Finally, I agreed, and I called Brian to set it up. He said he wasn't finished with his poster yet—he was supposed to be making one with lots of numbers and statistics about Australia—but I told him to just bring whatever he had and we could practice with that. We'd do it at my house, right after school.

· · · · ·

I asked Adam if he wanted to be in the audience too. So when school ended on Thursday, he and I walked out together, with Charity right behind us. I looked around for Brian, but he had disappeared.

Charity was looking too. "I hope Brian didn't forget," she said.

"He probably did," Adam said.

But then I spotted him, far down the block ahead of us, walking fast in his straight, stiff way, with his head down.

"Hey, Brian," I yelled.

He didn't turn around, so we hurried after him.

"Brian!"

This time he turned, and he waited for us to come closer.

"You're coming to my house, right?" I said.

"Yeah."

"OK."

All four of us walked the rest of the way to my house without saying much. I had a feeling that Adam and Charity were also wondering what Brian was going to do. I didn't have a clue about what Brian might be wondering about.

In my living room, Brian and I opened up our backpacks and got ready to practice, while Adam and Charity sat on the floor waiting.

I took out the cards with notes on what I was going to say and got the poster from my room. It was almost finished. I'd printed pictures of

Australia off the Internet—cities, desert land-scapes, crops, sheep farming, kangaroos and dingoes, Aborigines and their art—and I'd past-ed on typed paragraphs about all these things.

Brian's poster was supposed to be completely different. Mr. In had finally gotten him to do some real work on this project by telling him that since he loved numbers so much, he could make a poster with charts and graphs and stuff. Mr. In had helped him choose which numbers to include and what kind of graph to use.

I put my poster on the couch so everyone could see it. Then I stood beside it with my note cards in my hand. "I'm ready," I said.

Brian had a handful of note cards too, with four or five rubber bands wrapped tightly around them.

"Where's your poster?" I asked him.

"It's not done yet."

"I thought you were going to bring part of it so we could see how it's going."

His eyes shifted around the room, and he didn't answer.

I shrugged. "OK, I'll start."

I looked at my first note card and started talking. Pointing to the pictures on my poster, I explained all about Australia's climate, land, plants and animals, and agriculture and industry. I talked about the Aborigines too and how they were the original people of Australia and how today most of them are poor, but they still have some of their old traditions.

While I was talking, Lila came and stood in the doorway, watching. I didn't want her to listen. I glared at her but didn't interrupt what I was saying.

Finally, from the last card, I read my "hand-off sentence": "And now Brian will tell you about the government of Australia and give you some statistics about the people and the land."

Lila applauded, and Charity and Adam turned to look at her.

"You're not supposed to clap," I groaned.

"Nice job, Sylvan," she said. "Just try to look at your audience a little more, OK? Lots of eye contact."

"OK," I muttered.

There was silence for a minute while Brian fumbled with his cards, the rest of us watching him. He didn't look at us, just kept his head down and his eyes on the cards.

"Brian," Lila said gently, "would it be easier for you if I left, so you could practice your part just in front of the kids?"

"Yes," he said clearly, still without looking up.

"But we'll have visitors tomorrow, Brian," Charity said. "Sylvan's mom could be like a visitor."

"That's a good point, Charity," Lila said. "But for the very first time, I think we want to make it as easy as possible. I'll just go upstairs and let you kids go ahead."

Once she was gone, Brian finally got going.

"Australia. Government. Parliamentary democracy," he mumbled. "Six states and two territories. Capital. Canberra."

"You're just reading notes," Adam interrupted. "Say it like you're talking."

Brian blinked. "I *am* talking."

"No, like, *explain* it," Charity said. "Instead of 'government parliamentary democracy,' say, 'The government is a parliamentary democracy,' and then explain what that means."

Brian tried the first couple of note cards again and did a little better but only a little. He still sounded as stiff as a piece of wood. Then he just stopped.

"So . . . ," I said. "Are you going to talk about the poster next?"

"Yeah."

"What are you going to say?"

"I don't know. I can just show the poster."

Charity nodded. "But explain it, OK? Tell everybody what each part of it means."

"OK." He put his cards into his backpack.

I wondered if Brian understood why this was important. "We want to help Mr. In, right?" I said. "We want all the presentations to be really good, so Ms. Langley will know he's a great teacher."

He looked at me like I was an idiot. "I *know* that."

"Well, OK, I'm just reminding everybody."

Brian got his coat and backpack and headed for the front door.

"Bye, Brian," Charity said.

He didn't look back, but he said, "Oh. Bye," as if he remembered out of nowhere that that's what people say when they leave other people.

After Brian was gone, the three of us looked at one another.

"That was weird," Adam said.

"Yeah," I said. "And his part is going to be pretty lame tomorrow."

"Well, he did a little better the second time," Charity said hopefully.

"A *little*," Adam said.

"Maybe we should practice *our* presentation," she said.

Adam grinned. "Nah, I don't think we need to. Besides, I have to go. My mom wants me home." He put his coat on and picked up his backpack.

"See you tomorrow, Tree Boy. Bye, Charity." He went out the door, still grinning.

"See?" Charity burst out, as soon as the door closed behind Adam. "He's smirking about something. He's going to do something crazy tomorrow."

I had a feeling she was right.

chapter ten

CHARITY

"He's so cool," Deena whispered to me. "He doesn't even look nervous."

We had just finished morning meeting, and Mr. In was greeting Ms. Langley and the bald man at the door. Then he went to his desk, and they went to the back of the room, where two extra chairs had been placed.

Ms. Langley and the bald man were both smiling, looking around at us as they walked to the back. I glared at them. What were they doing, invading our class? Who gave them the right to judge Mr. In? We're the ones who know Mr. In, I thought. And we know he's great, and we won't let you take him away.

I wondered if Mr. Borthwick had read our petition, and why he hadn't sent us an answer. I hoped at least he'd be prepared, if Ms. Langley complained about Mr. In. He'd know she had to be wrong.

Mr. In was wearing his red tie with the flags on it—in honor of our international projects, he said. He started calling on people randomly to give their presentations, so no one would know when their turn was coming.

At first things went fine, and everybody was doing a good job. Take that, Ms. Langley, I thought. We all look pretty smart, and that's because Mr. In is a great teacher.

And then things started to go very, very wrong.

chapter eleven

SYLVAN

Rob and Melissa went first, talking about Nigeria. They had some cool pictures of the people
who live there, and I thought they did a pretty
good job. I looked back at Ms. Langley and the
bald man. They both had the same expression—
polite, paying attention, but not too interested.

Mr. In said thanks to Rob and Melissa, and
then he said, "Next, we'll have Sylvan and Brian
reporting on Australia."

I felt a little lurch in my stomach the second I

heard my name. If I'm kind of nervous, I thought, Brian must be shaking all over.

We went up to the front and set our posters on the easel, mine in front because I was going first. I still hadn't seen Brian's poster—couldn't even get a glimpse, because he put it on the easel backward.

"Australia is the only country that is also a continent," I began, and already I could feel my nervousness starting to fade. I explained about the land and the crops and sheep farms. I pointed out pictures of deserts and mountains and cities, including Sydney with the amazing opera house, like a row of white sails on the edge of the ocean. I talked about the Aborigines and how they live today, compared to the old ways. I told everyone what koalas like to eat and how far kangaroos can jump.

It had to have been the first time in my life I ever had fun talking in front of a class. And even though I never said so, I think everybody could tell that Australia was the place I most wanted to travel to, out of all the places in the world.

"OK, that's my report. And now"—my stomach lurched again—"Brian is going to tell you some important facts and numbers about Australia."

I looked at Ms. Langley and the bald man, and I swear they both perked up. They were watching Brian closely—nothing like the way they'd watched Rob and Melissa. I wondered, were they expecting Brian to do something weird? And if he did, would they blame it on Mr. In?

I took my poster and stood off to one side so that Brian could be next to the easel. He fumbled with the rubber bands around his note cards, peeling them off and putting them in his jeans pocket. Then he held the cards in front of him with both hands and opened his mouth. And closed it. He began twisting the cards in his hands.

The room was silent as everybody waited.

"You can do it, Brian," I said softly, trying to sound really quiet and calm, like Mr. In. "Like you did yesterday. Start with the part about the government."

Brian took a deep breath.

"The government of Australia is a parliamentary democracy," he read shakily from his first card. Then he took another big breath and kept going. He told us the names of the prime minister, the capital, and the states. He was almost mumbling, and he sounded as bored as everyone else probably felt. But at least he was doing it.

When he finished his list of facts, he turned his poster around so we could all see it.

It blew me away. I couldn't believe how good it was. There were two bar graphs and one of those pie-shaped things and another graph with lines and dots, all incredibly neat and colored with markers. And Brian actually explained them. I mean, he still didn't look at any of us, but he didn't mumble so bad. He even sounded a little proud when he pointed to each part of the poster.

"This shows how many people live in the cities and how many live in the country. And how almost all the people live in these two states.

"This shows how many people—I mean the percentage—that were born in another country. And how many are Aborigines."

Mr. In was right, I thought. He said we'd play to Brian's strengths, and this was what he meant. If you let Brian deal with the numbers—his favorite things—he could do a great job.

Besides how good the poster was, Brian was actually talking in front of the class. He was getting through this presentation almost like a normal kid. And that totally proved what a great teacher Mr. In was. I wondered if the bald man and Ms. Langley knew that or if they even had a clue.

As Brian and I went back to our seats, Adam gave us a thumbs-up, Charity smiled at us, and Mr. In said, "Excellent work, both of you." Then he called for the presentation on India.

"Hold my poster, OK?" Adam said to Charity as they stood up. Looking puzzled, she took the poster, and Adam pulled a box and a CD player from under his desk. They went to the front of the room, and he placed the CD player on Mr. In's desk and the box—carefully—on the floor.

I wondered what was in it—maybe whatever he got from his cousin? From the way Charity kept glancing at it, I was sure she didn't know either.

Charity went first. She told us about the Ganges River and cities like Mumbai and New Delhi, about the long history of India and how it had once been a colony of Great Britain, about rich people and poor people, and about the climate and the land. Her poster showed the clothes people wear in India, street scenes in Mumbai, and big buildings like the Taj Mahal.

Then it was Adam's turn. A lot of kids craned their necks for another look at the box by his feet, but he didn't pick it up. He just looked at his note cards and started talking about the Hindu religion and other religions in India. Then he talked about the caste system—how people are born into a certain group and that determines what sort of work they'll do when they grow up, and how they rank in society. There's even a group called the Untouchables, who are so low that other people won't have anything to do with them. He said the system is changing and isn't as strict as it used to be, but it's still important.

As he talked, Adam pointed to things on his poster, like a list of the castes and pictures of statues of Hindu gods. Then he pointed to one last picture. It showed a brown-skinned baby reaching his tiny hands toward a very big snake.

"OK, here's what's really cool," Adam said. "There are certain people who are snake charmers, and it's a family tradition. They keep cobras, which are really poisonous—deadly—and they put one in a basket, and when they play a flute in front of it, the snake raises its head and stares at the person and starts swaying along with the music."

Deena interrupted, looking outraged. "But that baby—won't the cobra kill it?"

"No, because its fangs have been taken out. See, the people don't want their children to be afraid of snakes, so they raise their kids around snakes that can't hurt them."

He bent down and picked up the box. "I couldn't bring a real cobra, but I brought something else to show you the basic idea."

He pushed a button on the CD player, and Indian music filled the air. Then he opened the box.

At first I couldn't see anything. And then a small, narrow head appeared over the side of the box. The snake rested its chin on the box's edge.

A couple of kids let out quick little shrieks. Adam was grinning. "So it goes like this," he said. Clutching the box with one hand, he reached in and pulled the snake's head up higher, so we could see its black body. Then he made the snake sway back and forth to the music, its head weaving side to side.

I started laughing, and so did almost everybody else.

But then I looked over at Brian. He was two rows to my left, almost at the front of the room, and just a few feet from the snake. He leaned back in his seat, both hands stiff in front of him, like he was trying to stay as far away from the snake as possible. It looked like another Brian blowup was about to happen.

I wasn't laughing anymore. If Brian freaked out, all the presentations would be ruined. And Ms. Langley would blame it on Mr. In. I waved my hand at Adam, trying to get his attention, so I could signal him to look at Brian.

But Adam was having way too much fun to notice. He brought the snake right up to Melissa, a couple seats away from Brian in the front row.

"Oooh, get *back*," she said, wrinkling her nose and pushing the box away.

More laughing. "Get *back*," Peter mimicked in a super-high voice. Even more laughing.

"OK, quiet down, please," Mr. In said. "Adam, let's wrap this up."

But instead, Adam moved closer to Lucy, who got grossed out if you even *mentioned* something like a worm or spider or snake. And Lucy was sitting next to Brian.

I totally wanted to see what Lucy would do with that snake in her face. But I never got the chance. Because the snake had had just about enough of being waved around like that. All of a sudden it whipped itself out of the box, slid through Adam's fingers, and landed right on Brian's desk.

"Heeeh," Brian wheezed, head back, hands clenched at his chest. "Heeh, heeeh." It was the weirdest sound, high-pitched and airy, like it was being squeezed out of his throat. I'd never heard a sound like that, but I knew what it meant—absolute terror.

A couple of girls squealed, Mr. In jumped up, and Adam lunged toward Brian's desk. But the snake—probably as terrified as Brian—slipped to the floor and shot toward the back of the room like a bullet. When it reached the last row, James leaned over and grabbed it behind the head, and held it up for everyone to see.

"Cool move, James," Kyle said. I had to agree, even though I couldn't stand either one of them.

Adam rushed back with his box, and he and James stuffed the snake inside. But the whole room was still going crazy. Kids jumped around, talking and yelling, pushing one another so they could see what was happening.

Mr. In was bending over Brian, whose hands were clutching the sides of his desk like he was on a roller coaster. He was still making that weird noise. Mr. In talked quietly to him, as though nothing else in the room existed.

I couldn't hear what Mr. In was saying, but I could sure hear Ms. Langley when she started to yell. "In your seats! Now!"

Maybe to Brian, Ms. Langley is worse than a snake. Because he jumped out of his seat, knocking the desk over, and ran out of the room. Mr. In ran after him.

Ms. Langley stalked over to the door and stared at us until every single kid was sitting down, mouth shut. Then she nodded to the bald man, and he followed her out of the room.

chapter twelve

CHARITY

I knew it. I knew Adam was planning to do something crazy, and he did. He and his snake had ruined everything, right in front of Ms. Langley.

As soon as Ms. Langley and the bald man left the room, one of the teacher's aides came in and sat down at Mr. In's desk. Her name was Ms. Russell. She wore dresses with bright flowers on them, and she looked as soft as a big pillow. She leaned back in Mr. In's chair with her arms crossed over her big chest.

"I hear you've had a little excitement in class today," she said. "Well, excitement's over. Mr. In is just getting Brian settled, and he'll be back in a few minutes. In the meantime, find yourself a book and let's all do some reading."

I don't think anybody felt like reading. I took a book out of my desk, but when I looked down at it, I didn't see the words. I just saw Ms. Langley's angry face and the bald man frowning and Brian running away.

When Mr. In came back, Brian wasn't with him. Ms. Russell left, and for a minute Mr. In just stood in front of the room, looking around at all of us.

Finally, he said, "This has been a very difficult day for Brian, so he's taking a break. He's gone home for the rest of the day. As you all know, noise and confusion are sometimes hard for him to handle."

He paused again, and this time he seemed to be speaking directly to Adam. "As you also know, Brian feels uncomfortable around all sorts of small creatures like insects. And reptiles."

"I didn't know he was afraid of snakes," Adam said in a small voice. He actually sounded sorry.

"Yes," said Mr. In. "And I realize that you didn't expect the snake to jump out and land on Brian's desk. Is your snake all right?"

"I think so."

"Could you bring it here, please?"

Mr. In moved over to his desk, and Adam followed him, carrying the box. Mr. In took the box, opened it, and looked inside. Then he taped it shut, very thoroughly.

"I'm glad to see you put some air holes in the lid, Adam," he said. "Your snake will be fine. Now please put this box in the closet. You can take it home at the end of the day."

Adam went to the closet, with all of us watching.

"Oh, and Adam?" said Mr. In.

Adam turned around, one hand on the closet doorknob and the other holding the box tight against his chest.

"Don't bring it back."

. . . . .

That afternoon I could hardly concentrate on anything we were doing in class. Ever since I'd watched Mr. In run after Brian, my heart had felt as low as the bottom of a river. First, Adam and his stupid snake turned everything into chaos—exactly what Ms. Langley hates the most. And then Brian got all upset and ran away. And Mr. In hadn't managed to stop any of it or calm Brian down. So our presentations, which were supposed to show what great work we could do with Mr. In's great teaching, had just convinced Ms. Langley that our class is out of control. She had something to use against him.

We had music that afternoon, but I didn't feel like singing. I barely opened my mouth.

When Faith and I got home, Mom was just getting back from the hospital, and right away she had to go out for groceries. Faith went straight to her room, like she always does. She likes quiet time by herself after school.

I went outside and played with JJ for a few minutes. His doggy grin and soft ears and his tail that never stopped wagging always made me feel a little better. But it was too cold to stay outside for long.

I brought my bag of books to the dining table, got some crackers and milk, and started on my homework. I worked slowly through math, social studies, and science, then heard the slam of the truck door—one of the other painters dropping Dad off. But he didn't come in right away, and I went to the back door to look for him.

He was throwing a stick for JJ to chase. He wore his winter jacket but no hat, even though a few flakes of snow were drifting around. He still looked like Bwana Simba, I thought, with his thick hair blown back by the wind and his strong arm throwing the stick to the farthest corner of the yard.

JJ raced after the stick again and again, barking joyfully.

Dad didn't look joyful at all. He looked like a person doing something necessary but not fun, like a set of push-ups. He looked like he was thinking hard.

I still had my coat on. I went out the door and put my arm around his waist.

"Miss Charity!" he said with a smile, but his eyes were still far away.

JJ came rushing back and dropped his stick, and I hugged him and petted his rough coat. When he licked my face, I couldn't help laughing a little.

"How was school?"

I told him about the presentations and the snake and Brian getting upset and running away, and Ms. Langley and the stranger watching everything.

Dad looked amused but impressed too. "That's quite an eventful day."

Sudden tears stung my eyes. "No," I said, "it was a *terrible* day."

Dad gave the stick one last toss and said, "Let's go inside and have a talk about this."

He made us hot chocolate while I shared my awful fear that Ms. Langley would fire Mr. In. A few tears spilled over as I tried to explain how we'd all wanted to make Mr. In look good.

Dad shook his head, putting a cup on the table in front of me. "You're worrying too much, Charity. Sounds like the main problem today was that kid Brian. No principal is going to fire a teacher because of an incident like that. More likely she's thinking about whether Brian needs some kind of special help."

"Oh," I said with a sniffle. I wasn't sure he was right—after all, he didn't know Ms. Langley, with her hawk eyes and her crocodile smile—but his calm voice made me feel a little better.

"Mr. In means a lot to you, doesn't he?" Dad asked.

I nodded.

"Why is that?"

"Well, he's a really good teacher, and he's so nice."

"Nice how?"

I frowned. "Dad, why do you ask so many questions?"

"Because that's how you get answers. So tell me how Mr. In has been nice to you."

I didn't want to explain Mr. In to my father.

But he kept asking questions, and finally the words started coming out. I told him how strange I felt in school, especially at first. How kids laughed at me for shaking hands with the teacher and things like that. I told him that Mr. In had explained to the kids that in some schools that's how everybody does things and that he gave me a chance to tell the class about Shibuye and how after that most of the kids seemed to accept me a little more. I said that Mr. In made me feel like a special person, a smart person, not a weird girl who didn't know how to act.

Dad listened to all this, and then he said, "You've had a hard time adjusting to this place, haven't you?"

I nodded and held onto my warm cup, staring down at the tiny marshmallows drifting like sailboats on a tiny sea.

"Has your faith helped you through this?"

In our family we'd always talked a lot about faith. When I was little, my parents always told me about God's love for me. They said that having faith meant you could always feel that love, even when things went wrong and that when you were upset or confused, you could always ask God what to do.

But this time Dad wasn't telling me what faith could do for me. He was asking.

"Well . . ." I wasn't sure how to answer. "I felt a little better after I prayed about it. But it didn't make the problems go away."

He nodded slowly but didn't say anything. He seemed to have run out of questions.

· · · · ·

The next day was Saturday, and I woke up to an amazing sight. Snow! Millions and millions of white flakes floating to Earth—perfect snowflakes to catch on a tongue or on a dark sleeve where you could see the shapes, like bits of lace.

Yesterday the backyard had been all scraggly with pale grass and dead leaves and sticks. Now it was pure white. Every tree branch, from the largest limb to the smallest twig, was a dark line with a white line on top of it.

When Faith looked out the living room window, she said, "Christmas! It's Christmas!"

"No, silly," I said. "It's two or three more weeks till Christmas."

"Oh. Well, let's go outside."

We scrambled into our brand-new snow pants and coats and boots and hats and mittens. The second we got outside, we stopped and leaned our heads back and stared up into that endless field of drifting flakes.

Then we shuffled our boots in it, running across the yard and glancing back at deep footprints. We scooped up handfuls of snowflakes and flung them into the air. I showed Faith how to make a snowman, because I remembered perfectly and she didn't remember at all.

After a while Faith wanted to go inside and get warm, but I didn't. I wanted to walk around the neighborhood and see how different everything looked. Mom said it was all right, so I went. Everything was clean and beautiful, as if some fairy had transformed the world overnight. Little pyramids of snow topped off fence posts and chimneys. Some people were shoveling sidewalks or sweeping off steps and porches, and they smiled at me as I went past.

I came to Brian Laidlaw's house, with the trampoline in the side yard. Brian was standing beside it. He looked lost or confused. For a second I wondered if he was still upset about the day before, but then I saw that his trampoline was covered with snow. He probably couldn't use it like that. Maybe that had made him sad.

"Hi, Brian," I said.

"Hi."

"Can't you use your trampoline?"

He shook his head. But just then his mother came out of the house with two brooms. "OK, Brian, now we'll get the snow off," she said cheerfully. Then, seeing me, she said, "Oh, hello. Brian, will you introduce me to your friend?"

He mumbled something I couldn't hear.

"Charity? Oh yes, you do look familiar. You're in Brian's class, aren't you?"

"Yes." I didn't recognize her at all. She was short and roundish, with very short gray hair.

"Would you like to go on the trampoline, once we get it swept off?"

I'd never been on anything like that, although I'd seen Brian on it sometimes when I was walking by or passing in the car. But it looked like fun. "Umm, I guess I could try it," I said.

Then I thought maybe I should have said "no, thanks," because Brian didn't look happy at all. But his mother said, "Great!" She seemed so delighted that I had a feeling she really wanted Brian to have someone to do stuff with. She climbed onto the trampoline through a flap in the netting that surrounded it and called to Brian to follow her. In a few minutes they had swept off the snow.

Once Brian's mother climbed out again, Brian began jumping. Straight up and down, over and over. At first his face was blank and stiff, but slowly he seemed to relax, and his arms moved more, until he was almost smiling. His mother and I just stood there and watched. It was strange that he didn't say anything to me, like "come on up," or "you can have a turn in a minute." But I didn't really expect him to say what other kids would say.

Finally, his mom said, "Brian, could you give Charity a turn?"

He bounced a few more times, then stopped. He moved to one side of the trampoline, away from the flap.

"Go ahead, Charity," his mother said. "Just jump up and down, though. Don't try any flips or somersaults—that's our main safety rule."

The trampoline wobbled under my knees. Carefully I stood up, moving my feet apart to stay balanced.

Then Brian bent his knees and launched himself high into the air. The trampoline rippled like an earthquake. My feet flew out from under me, and my rear end hit the surface and bounced a couple of times. For a second I couldn't find my breath, and then I laughed and scrambled to my feet. I started jumping and bouncing all over the place. I kept falling, but I didn't care. I felt wild and silly and giddy—this was the most fun I'd had since we moved back to America.

Brian stared at me with a surprised expression. He must have made me fall on purpose.

Maybe he was hoping I'd go away so he could have the trampoline all to himself. But jumping felt so wonderful, I didn't care.

For a while Brian just stood at the edge, holding onto the netting and bending his knees as the surface moved, watching me in a not-so-friendly way. But then he moved closer to the middle, and I moved over a little too. Both of us started to bounce again. This was harder, and I fell down a lot. But falling never hurt! We got into a rhythm, one of us up while the other one was down.

I tried to look straight up into the sky while I jumped, without getting dizzy and falling. Then I heard something and looked down. Melissa and Lucy were standing on the sidewalk, staring at us and giggling. When they saw me look, they hurried away, laughing so hard they kept bumping against each other.

I messed up my jump, and Brian and I both fell down.

"I'm sorry," I said. I was thinking I must have looked really stupid, bouncing up and down with weird Brian. Maybe I'd go home.

"They're *stupid*," Brian said, standing up.

I was surprised to hear the same word that was in my own head. Except he said it about them, not me.

I stood up shakily. Maybe I didn't care if they laughed. Maybe I *wouldn't* go home.

I took a couple of small, slow bounces off the tips of my toes, and so did Brian. Gradually we began to jump higher and faster, and then we were bouncing as hard as ever, zooming off the trampoline into the sky.

chapter thirteen

SYLVAN

When the bell rang at the end of that crazy Friday, Mr. In came over to me and said, "Would you stay a minute, Sylvan?"

Surprised, I just nodded. Mr. In went back to his desk. Adam shrugged and hurried out with everyone else. Soon there were only two people left—me, standing with my jacket on, and Mr. In, leaning back in his desk chair and smiling.

"That was quite a day, wasn't it?" he said.

"Yeah, it was wild."

"I just wanted to tell you what a good presentation you gave—you and Brian. And what a great job you did helping Brian get through this."

"He made a cool poster," I said. "And he talked in front of everybody."

Mr. In nodded. "Those were very big steps for him. And you deserve a lot of credit for encouraging him."

"I didn't think it was going to work out—me and Brian being partners, I mean. I thought he just wouldn't do anything. But you said I was the one who could work with him best. So I tried. Only . . ." I didn't know quite how to say it.

"Only what?"

"Well, I just wondered why you said that. I mean, I was never all that nice to Brian. I wasn't mean or anything, but I didn't, like, hang around and talk to him. So—why did you say I'd be good for him?"

Mr. In just looked at me seriously for a moment. Then he smiled. "Because I knew you could be."

That didn't make any sense. How could he know what was in me? He didn't know me that well.

"You mean, you thought I was kind of like Brian?"

"No, not that exactly. But I believed you'd be able to understand, a little, what it's like to *be* Brian."

"Oh." I thought this over. "But I don't really understand him. I can hardly ever figure out what he's thinking. All I know is, a lot of things scare him—especially loud things and things that might crawl on you. And I'm pretty sure he *knows* he's different."

"I'm sure he does," Mr. In said. He smiled again. "But then, everyone's different, one way or another."

chapter fourteen

CHARITY

On Monday Brian was back in school but quieter than ever. He scrunched down at his desk like he was trying to make himself invisible. Sometimes you couldn't see his face, only the top of his neatly cut white-blond hair. Once I saw him cover his ears with his hands, very lightly at first, then pressing harder, as if he was testing how much he could still hear that way.

The whole day, I never saw the bald man or even Ms. Langley. I wished I knew what they said to each other after they left our class.

Then on Tuesday, at morning meeting, Mr. In said in a serious voice, "I have some news to share with you."

I felt a sharp, scared feeling in my stomach. Ms. Langley couldn't have fired him already— could she? But that wasn't the news.

"Brian is going to be leaving us, to go to a different school," he went on.

We all stared at him and at Brian.

"Brian," Mr. In said, "I'm really going to miss you. But you'll be in Ms. Bellini's class at South Ridge, and she's terrific. I think you'll like her." He looked around at all of us. "We'll have a good-bye party for Brian at the end of the day tomorrow, since that will be his last day. I'll bring snacks. But remember, everybody—it's going to be a *quiet* party, because that's the way Brian likes it. OK?"

. . . . .

"Hey, Brian," I heard Sylvan say as we all rushed out of school at the end of the day. "So you're going to South Ridge."

"Yeah."

"Do you *want* to go?"

"No," Brian said, studying the slushy pavement in front of him as we walked. "I want to stay with Mr. In."

"Oh, that's too bad," I put in. He really did look sad. "I wish you could stay."

"Are your parents making you switch?" Sylvan asked.

"Yes. And Ms. Langley. And Mr. Herkimer."

"Who's Mr.—what did you say?"

"Mr. Herkimer."

"Who's he?" I asked.

"He's—I don't know. He figures out what school people should go to."

"You aren't moving, are you?" Sylvan asked.

"No. I live at 423 Oakwood Street." He said it in a funny way, almost like a robot.

We came to the corner where Sylvan had to turn toward his house.

"Hey, Brian?" Sylvan said. "I'm glad you did the Australia project with me. You were cool."

"Yeah, you were," I said.

"Oh." Brian looked confused.

"So anyway, I'll see you in the neighborhood sometime, OK?" Sylvan grinned. "On your trampoline, right?"

Brian nodded seriously. "I still have my trampoline."

We said good-bye to Sylvan, and a block later I had to turn onto Bradley Street. "Bye, Brian," I said. "I hope you like your new school."

"I still have one more day in Mr. In's class," he said.

"I know. See you tomorrow."

·····

On the first day after Brian left, his empty desk looked strange. The top was clean, and even his name card was gone.

We had art that morning, and when we came back to the classroom, Mr. In was standing at the front of the room with an envelope in one hand. His red tie had little white rectangles on it, almost like name cards without names. He waited for us to sit down and get quiet.

"I received a very interesting letter a couple of days ago," he said. "The district superintendent, Mr. Borthwick, wrote to me. He enclosed a copy of a letter that he'd received—from you."

Mr. In sat down on the front of his desk, holding the envelope, and looked around the room. "It's a very well-written letter. In fact, I was proud to see that my students can write so well. And I was touched by all the nice things you said about me. And even more touched that you would take the trouble to write this letter, get everyone to sign it, and send it to Mr. Borthwick."

He opened the envelope and unfolded the papers inside. "But there's one thing I don't understand. It says here, 'Please don't listen to anyone who says he shouldn't teach here. We want to have Mr. Inayatullah for our teacher all year.'" He looked up, and little wrinkles of puzzlement lined his forehead. "I would like to know why you wrote that—why you thought I might be leaving."

I didn't give anyone else a chance to answer—the words just burst out of me. "Because Ms. Langley keeps coming in and watching you! And she's so mean, and—"

"And she fired Ms. Day," Deena said. "And she was always coming in and watching her too."

"And that man," I went on in a rush. "The one who came with her. I heard him talking to her about not being prepared and things like that."

The puzzled lines disappeared from Mr. In's smooth forehead. "Oh, I see. Yes, I see how you could think that. But they weren't here to evaluate me. They were here for entirely different reasons."

Relief flooded into me, but it was mixed with confusion.

Adam asked the question that was in my mind. "So why *did* they come all those times?"

"Well, the visitor, Mr. Herkimer, is a psychologist who works for the school district. I believe he spends three days a week at South Ridge. He and Ms. Langley wanted to see how

Brian was getting along here. They've been discussing with his parents whether another school might work better for him."

He shook his head. "I was hoping to keep Brian. He's made some real progress here."

"But South Ridge is a regular school too," Melissa said. "I mean, it's not a school for—for—"

"For kids who need special help?" Mr. In said, and Melissa nodded.

"You're right—it is a regular school, but it's much larger than Henderson, and it has some special programs that might be good for Brian. So I can understand the decision, even though, as I said, I was hoping to keep him."

He smiled at us. "Working with someone like Brian can expand your mind. That's why I was hoping he could stay—not just for his own sake but for me. And for all of you."

. . . . .

That night, after we'd had dinner and I had finished all my homework, I sat down at the dining table to write a letter.

Dear Grace,

My teacher isn't leaving after all. I was wrong—the mean headmistress was not trying to send him away. I'm so happy about that. Now if only my—

I was going to write something like "if only my father could be the way he used to be." But I stopped just in time—because just then my father walked into the room. He put his hands on my shoulders and kissed the top of my head.

"What are you doing?" he asked.

"Writing to Grace."

He pulled out a chair and sat down. "You feeling better about school now?"

I'd already told him about how Mr. In had explained why Ms. Langley had been coming to our class. "Sure. At least I don't have to worry about Mr. In anymore."

"What else do you have to worry about?"

"Oh, nothing."

"Is that so?"

I looked away. "Well, sure."

He leaned forward with his elbows on the table to get a better look at me. "You don't worry about having a father who's gone from a minister to an unbeliever? A father who paints houses all day and doesn't say much when he comes home?"

"Well, I do, a little," I admitted.

"That's what I thought." He laid his hands palm down on the table between us and just looked at them for a moment, as though he was deciding what to say next. There was a streak of blue paint on the back of his left hand. "Charity, this has been a tough time for me. Things went so badly at Shibuye that I started questioning everything I'd believed. And I still don't have answers. I don't even know if I'll ever be a Christian again."

I kept very still, just watching him. I felt like we were both balancing on a wire. How could someone who had been so sure of everything now be so full of doubt? If he could change so much, what was *I* supposed to believe?

He must have known what was going on

inside me. "Charity, just because I'm thinking this way doesn't mean there's anything wrong with you believing, the same way you always have. Same for Mom and Faith too. People are different. It's okay for people to believe different things."

He paused, then went on. "Maybe it's even okay to *change* what you believe now and then."

I liked that idea. I liked it more, the more I thought about it. Because it meant you didn't have to be right all the time. You could relax a little.

I smiled at him.

"So, can you handle this, Charity? The new Dad? Not a minister, but not angry and upset anymore either. I still think about all that, but right now my main goal is just to make an honest living and love my family."

"That's good," I said. "That's *cool*."

He squeezed my arm. "Thanks. And meanwhile, you can quit worrying. I'll figure things out. But whatever's going on with me, I'll always take care of you and Faith and Mom."

He sounded sure, and I felt sure too.

"Yes, Bwana Simba," I said, and he actually laughed.

chapter fifteen

SYLVAN

Lila had another protest thing going on—she was part of a group that was picketing a pizza place downtown, because they didn't treat their workers right. I hoped she wasn't going to make me be part of it. I walked super slow on the way home from school.

I was feeling pretty good, aside from dreading getting home. It was great to know that Mr. In wasn't in trouble. I was kind of sorry that Brian was gone—I mean, I'd actually started to like him. I felt good about helping him do the project, especially when I remembered the nice things Mr. In had said about me.

Snow was still hanging around from last weekend, dirty and old-looking. It was trampled down whichever way you looked. I wished we'd get new snow, so everything would look clean and white again, and the sledding would be good.

When I got home, I didn't go inside at first. I went to the backyard to see the chickens. I closed the gate behind me, then poked my head into the coop, where the hens were all huddled together to keep warm. They fluttered and cackled until they realized it was only me. The smell in there was pretty bad, but I didn't mind too much. I petted Zsa Zsa and Drucilla and Josephine, but Esmeralda and Eustacia—the big white ones— stayed in the back, perched side by side. They watched me the whole time, but they weren't about to leave their cozy spot just to be friendly.

Before leaving I checked their water bowl— it's heated so that it doesn't freeze—and made sure the loose plastic at one corner of the coop was tucked in tight.

At the front door I found Zachary. His orange fur was fluffed out to keep him warm. He gave a loud meow and rubbed against me, and darted inside the second I opened the door.

I couldn't even sneak up to my room, because Lila was right there, sitting with a book in the living room. Zachary jumped in her lap, knocking the book to the floor.

"Hi, Sylvan," she said, rubbing Zachary's head. "How was your day?"

"Good." I dropped my backpack and took off my coat.

"You might want to keep that coat on."

I hung it up anyway. "Why?"

"We have someplace to go." She had that glint in her eye, the way she looks when she's on a mission, like she's ready to go out and face the enemy.

"Not that pizza place," I groaned.

"You got it."

"No way. Lila, I *really* don't want to go."

"Sylvan, do you know what this is all about? These people—the cooks and waiters and delivery people—make very little money. And their boss has been making them work overtime without paying them and saying he'll fire them if they don't do it. It's totally unfair. And we're going to be there with signs, telling people not to go there for pizza until this guy cleans up his act."

I crouched down and opened my backpack and started taking out books and notebooks. "Yeah, I know he's a bad guy and everything, but I have a ton of homework. I'll just stay here and do homework the whole time, I promise."

"Wait just a minute," she said, shifting Zachary into her chair as she stood up. Her voice got higher. "Don't you care about these poor people who are being mistreated?"

Of course that made me feel guilty. And mad. "Well, yeah, sure, but..." I stood up to face her—and hey, I thought, I was almost as tall as her. "Look, Lila, that's your kind of project, and it's cool, but—it's not my project. I just want to be a normal kid."

"You *are* a normal kid. Doing something like this doesn't make you abnormal. It just makes you more responsible and aware and involved than most kids."

I rolled my eyes. She glared at me and kept on talking. "That's *better* than normal. Who knows what normal is, anyway?"

"Well, it's not normal for a kid to stand on the street waving a big sign!" I yelled. "People already think I'm not normal, because—because of last year—and the thing with the tree—and—"

She stared at me while I fumbled for words, and her voice came out quieter this time. "Sylvan, getting upset and acting out after your parents split up is about the most normal thing a kid can do. It happens all the time. I understood that, your father understood it, your teachers understood it." She put her hands on my shoulders. "And look how you've come through! You're doing great this year. You're a lot calmer, you're getting along with other kids, and your grades are good. You've adjusted really well."

I wriggled my shoulders out from under her

hands, but I was thinking about what she'd said about kids getting in trouble after their parents split up. It was nice to think that some of those grown-ups who were always frowning at me really did understand what was going on. Like maybe they knew I'd get over it.

And maybe I really was a normal kid—just like I'd been saying all along. A normal, average, everyday kid.

But that didn't change my plans for the afternoon.

"OK, OK, maybe I'm normal. But I still don't want to go to a protest!"

She folded her arms and looked me over. "Let me see that so-called ton of homework."

I bent down obediently to get it. But I had to hide my grin, because I knew I'd won, and she was just stalling before she agreed to let me stay. I know Lila pretty well. In fact, she may even be a normal mom. Sort of.

· · · · ·

Christmas is only about a week away—the first Christmas since Will and Lila separated. The plan is for me and Justin to stay at Lila's on Christmas Eve, and the next morning Will is going to come over to eat breakfast and open presents with us. Then he'll leave, and we'll hang around with Lila, but that night we'll go over to Will's place to sleep.

It's definitely going to be weird and sometimes maybe sad too. I'm really glad Justin is going to be there with me, at both places.

And two days after Christmas I'm going skiing with Adam and his family. We'll get up really early and drive to this slope in the mountains. I hardly ever get to go skiing, and I can't wait.

Charity invited me to go with her family to the Christmas Eve service at her church. At first I thought, no way. A normal kid like me doesn't hang around with a kid like Charity—especially not to go to church.

And then I thought, but Charity *is* normal, just a little different.

And then I thought, What exactly does "normal" mean, anyway?

Charity said, "Come on, you always say you

want to go to foreign countries and see new things. This will be like a foreign country, for you."

She had a point. In fact, I've never gone to a church in my whole life. It's just something Will and Lila don't do. And I'm kind of curious about it.

So I said yes to Charity. And I'd already said yes to Adam about the ski trip.

With ten whole days of winter break, I might even stop by Brian's house one day and see if he'll let me go on the trampoline with him.

I don't know if you'd call Brian exactly normal, but I like him.

I also said yes to me—yes, I can handle this new kind of mixed-up Christmas with my mixed-up family. Because like I keep saying, I am a normal kid.

Whatever that means.

ABOUT THE AUTHOR

Elizabeth Holmes is the author of two other middle-grades novels—*Pretty Is* and *Tracktown Summer*—and two books of poetry. She lives in Ithaca, New York, with her husband, two sons, and three cats. She believes the whole family is just about normal. Visit her online at elizabethholmesbooks.com.